HORIZON
THE GAME

A small group of survivors steps from
the wreckage of a plane . . .
And you're one of them.

JOIN THE RACE FOR SURVIVAL!

1. Download the app or go to **scholastic.com/horizon**
2. Log in to create your character.
3. Go to the Sequencer in your home camp.
4. Input the above musical sequence.
5. Claim your prize!

Available for tablet, phone, and browser.
scholastic.com/horizon

A WARP IN TIME

JUDE WATSON

SCHOLASTIC INC.

Library of Congress Control Number: 2017953043

ISBN 978-1-338-18701-4

10 9 8 7 6 5 4 3 2 1   18 19 20 21 22

Book design by Abby Dening

First edition, February 2018

Printed in the U.S.A.   37

Scholastic US: 557 Broadway · New York, NY 10012
Scholastic Canada: 604 King Street West · Toronto, ON M5V 1E1
Scholastic New Zealand Limited: Private Bag 94407 · Greenmount, Manukau 2141
Scholastic UK Ltd.: Euston House · 24 Eversholt Street · London NW1 1DB

To all the kids in the band

NEWSLINE: UTQIAĠVIK, ALASKA

Townspeople in this northernmost city in Alaska reported a strange sighting earlier this week. An otherworldly light in the sky was observed in the northeast, according to several persons who witnessed it that afternoon.

"I was walking my dog, Pokey, and I saw it light up the sky," Bert Tremundo said as he exited Mab's Café. "It was like a bright column reaching up into the clouds. Or maybe down. Hard to say."

"We had to look away it was so bright," said MaryAnn Beeks, the owner of Mab's Café. "We see a lot of strange things in the sky this far north, but this one took the salmon cake."

The sighting prompted a flurry of tweets in this Arctic city, as well as calls to law enforcement.

"You'd think folks would get used to the northern lights, but they don't," Sheriff Gene Toomer said. "We get calls all the time, mostly from tourists and crazies getting all spooky hoo-ha on us."

"I know what northern lights are—I've seen 'em enough times," William "Bootlace" Jones said, when told of the sheriff's comments. "Somebody should do his job instead of calling people names."

The United States Navy characterized the phenomenon as falling "space junk," which most likely splashed harmlessly into the Arctic Ocean.

1

Javi

The smoke was gone. It had been there, a plume reaching into the sky, and now there was just endless gray. Javi felt hope drain from his body. They had been low on food rations for so long now—if you could even count sour candy as food—that he wondered if they had hallucinated the smoke.

Had they imagined the music as well?

That had stopped, too, as soon as they stepped into the forest. A high, piping noise like a flute, mingling with deeper, mournful notes. Then silence.

"Birds," Yoshi had said. Always the first one to squash a hopeful sign, always the last one to get a joke. It was lucky he was incredibly brave and saved people, Javi thought, or else he'd be *completely* annoying.

There had been a burst of Japanese from Akiko and Kira, but when they all looked to Yoshi to translate, he'd just said, "They agree."

"If they ever offer you a job at the UN as a translator, the world is in trouble," Javi had said.

Yoshi grunted in reply, but Kira had grinned at Javi. She didn't speak English, but he could tell she understood a good burn.

"Ready?" his best friend, Molly, asked, in the lead as usual.

Not really. Javi shifted his feet. He was supposed to be her deputy. Her second-in-command, her backup. Right now he *felt* like backing up. All the way back in time to the moment before they all boarded the plane in New York so that he could yell *Stop!* as soon as their feet hit the Jetway.

Aero Horizon Flight 16 was supposed to have been the start of an amazing adventure. The Robotics Club at Brooklyn Science and Tech were on their way to prizes and glory at the Robot Soccer World Championship in Tokyo, Japan. Go, Team Killbot! Javi had been so excited he could barely eat the big pancake-and-egg breakfast his mom had made him.

His stomach lurched. He'd forgotten how empty it was. *Don't think about food. It just reminds you of home.*

Instead of adventure, he'd gotten disaster. The plane had broken apart in midair, the roof peeling back like an anchovy can (*don't think about food*). Javi still remembered his terror, how even squeezing his eyes closed hadn't shut out the strange bright light that had invaded the cabin. That light seemed to judge him somehow, to choose him, to *save* him— and doom the hundreds of other passengers who were sucked out of the cabin.

Finally, the plane had crash-landed—except it hadn't really crash-landed, as Molly had pointed out. They had seemed to *glide* down, smashing through treetops and coming to rest in the middle of what should have been the Arctic but was a red-tinged jungle full of aggressive vines and terrible birds with beaks like razors.

In fact, the jungle was so strange they'd had to wonder if they were even still on Earth. It wasn't until some of them saw the stars that they knew they were. The Big Dipper was there. The North Star. If only it could lead them home.

Ahead of them now were soaring trees, not like the ones in the red jungle, twisted and dense, but solid trunks spaced apart with branches that spread wide. The leaves were as big as dinner plates. The air smelled fresh and reminded him of cool water and shade. Far in the distance rose a ridge studded with needle-laden trees, looking like an overturned hairbrush against the gray sky. It was the first place that looked like . . . well, *Earth*.

He took a deep breath. To get away from the treacherous sucking sand of the desert was a relief he felt in his bones. He had been through the worst day of his life, but now it was a new day, and he was still standing.

He looked over at Akiko and Kira, the Japanese sisters who had been on the plane with them. Like Yoshi, they weren't on the robotics team. They were just traveling home from their school in Switzerland.

He pointed to his nose and gestured at the woods. "It smells good," he said.

They both nodded.

"Strange color," Kira said. He looked at the woods again. Kira was an artist. She saw color more precisely, Javi guessed. She was right. The leaves were dark green, but they had a bluish tinge. More the dark of the ocean right before a storm.

"Ao," he agreed. *Blue.*

"Oliver would love to see this," Anna said. "It feels like home."

Javi swallowed hard. Out of hundreds of passengers, only eight kids had survived. And now they were down to six. Caleb had died, crushed in a low-gravity field. And Oliver— two years younger than they were, scared and determined . . . now he was gone, too.

Oliver had been sucked under the blood sand, but he had returned, more like a robot than the kid they knew. He had come back to encourage them to keep going and then had sunk under the sand again. They didn't know if he was alive or dead.

"We're going to see him again," Molly said. "He said we were."

"But he wasn't really Oliver when he said that," Anna said. "He was obviously being controlled somehow."

"We know, Anna. We were there," said Molly.

"He was like a zombie. Like the walking dead."

Leave it to Anna to say what they were all trying not to think.

"Enough!" Molly snapped. "Oliver is alive, period. Now let's head in the direction of the music we heard."

"Birds," Yoshi said, because he wasn't about to change his mind.

Javi didn't even know if Molly meant what she said. She had made the decision to stop searching for Oliver in the first place. Now she didn't even look sad. She looked as though she'd just designed a gyro gear program for a robot and it hadn't worked. Like your friend getting sucked under blood sand was an annoyance you could fix if you put your head down and worked harder.

Did he still know his best friend? She was so into being their leader now, so intent on their mission to get to the end of the valley, that he had a feeling she'd say anything to keep them moving.

Before the plane crash she'd just been Molly—smart, funny, intense, maybe a little bossy sometimes. They'd shared a love for robotics and double chocolate milk shakes. After her dad died, Javi's family had drawn her in, the way you'd fold your little brother into your coat to keep him warm.

Sometimes on Saturday mornings he'd stumble-bumble his way into the kitchen, still half-asleep, and Molly would already be there, kicking the table leg and on her second helping of pancakes.

When they'd crashed into this insane valley, he hadn't even wondered who should be the leader. Molly had taken charge right away. By the time she got to the bottom of the emergency slide she had probably cooked up three scenarios on How to Fix This.

Except it wasn't fixable.

Was Molly? She'd been bitten by a prehistoric-looking bird with a long razor beak that had torn the flesh on her shoulder. The wound was strange and Molly had nearly died. Now she was as strong as ever, but . . . different.

He could feel it. Something was missing, or maybe something had been . . . added? And it kept getting worse. The horrors they'd seen here had changed all of them, he knew. Molly most of all. He didn't want his best friend to change too much.

Leaves rustled around them. There was a narrow path to follow, overgrown in places. The path wasn't straight; it ran up and down the slight hills and, from what he could see, it twisted through the woods. Occasionally, a narrower path would run off in a different direction. They came to several forks and Molly just plunged on.

"Where are we going?" Yoshi asked. "The sound came from the left."

"We did go left," Molly said.

"Yes, but then we turned right again," Anna said.

"We came from that direction. See?" Molly turned and gestured.

"No," Anna said. "You're wrong."

Anna never said, "You *might* be wrong," or "I *think* it's this way."

They stopped.

Molly held up a hand. "Wait. I hear that sound again."

Now Javi could hear it, too, something high and piping.

"Birds," Yoshi said. He adjusted the Japanese sword he wore strapped to his back.

"No bird." Akiko smiled. "Mozart," she said.

Molly

The music swelled, louder now. Everyone froze, then lifted their chins, mouths open as if they could catch the tune and drink it down like water. How long had it been since they'd heard music? Since the plane when they had their earbuds in, or maybe the radio as their parents drove them to the airport.

Molly felt it in her body, each beat of the delirious melody. Rising and falling, looping and rushing and slowing. Her brain flooded, overflowing. Music! That meant . . .

"People," Anna breathed.

With that one word, the spell broke, and they all took off, running flat out, whooping.

Except for Molly.

Molly couldn't move.

The music had stunned her. Like she'd been hit on the head

and fallen into a dream. That pure melody of joy, with something sad underneath, like a steady pulse of sorrow. First she'd thought of Oliver, the grief at losing him still raging. Then, without warning, she was plunged into a memory of her dad.

It wasn't even a special memory. It was an everyday memory. The door to her room opening and him touching her hair and saying, "Hey, bug. Rise and shine."

And suddenly she heard his voice, the teasing and softness in it. She *heard him.*

Which was ridiculous, because number one, she was lost in a weird valley that made no sense, and number two, her dad was dead.

Tears swam in her eyes and she wiped them away but they kept on coming, even as she ran after the others. She was last. She was never last! Even Javi was ahead of her, and basically? She could probably beat Javi in a footrace if she *hopped* the entire way.

Yoshi was far in the lead now. He was the fastest runner, Anna right behind, and the sisters at her heels. They disappeared around a curve and were swallowed up by the woods.

Molly felt a deep loneliness overtake her. For this moment, she was alone. Her fingers pressed against her shoulder, right where her wound was. It didn't hurt, but it felt like there was something beneath the skin. Like an *object* lodged there, softer than bone. Scar tissue?

Ever since she'd been bitten by the dreadful duck of doom,

she'd been changing. Her hearing was sharper, her upper-body strength had increased. Good things, but strange. Troubling. And the nightmares . . . those never let up.

Who wouldn't have nightmares after a plane crash? It probably had nothing to do with the bite.

Molly caught a flash of something: a yellow flower on a bush. While she watched, petals opened, then closed. The flower drooped, and then fell.

What was that?

The back of her neck prickled. She was used to seeing weird things in this valley. This felt different. Maybe because the woods had felt so safe. It had been a long time since she'd gulped down the fresh smell of earth and leaves. She had another sharp, clear memory of being in Prospect Park on one of those first springlike days. In the shade it was cool, but in the sun she threw off her jacket and she and Javi tossed a Frisbee . . .

She heard Anna shout in surprise and fear, and the sound yanked Molly out of that clear memory and straight back to the present.

She began to run.

When she rounded the curve, Anna was standing stock-still, staring down. Yoshi was gone.

Anna

Anna had adjusted to being in a place where, at any moment, something could go really, really wrong. At this point she thought nothing could surprise her. She'd always be prepared.

Not so.

One moment Yoshi had been there; the next, he was gone.

Her heart leaping in panic, she ran ahead and stopped just in time. Yoshi had fallen into a deep pit.

She peered over the edge. Yoshi looked up at her, his face tight and angry.

"I crashed through some kind of platform," he said.

"Maybe you should rethink this whole thing about always going first." Anna glanced around, taking in the pit's concealed edges. "It looks like sticks and leaves were arranged over the hole. That's an old trick."

Yoshi's face reddened. "And I fell for it?"

"Well, you *did* fall," Anna said. Sometimes kids at school called her mean. She wasn't mean. She just saw reality clearly, and she shared it without dusting it in sugar and rainbows first.

One day, when Anna was in first grade, she'd come home crying after her best friend had suddenly refused to sit with her at lunch. Her mother had tried to comfort her. "When someone asks you if you like their dress, say yes," she said.

Anna had sniffed, tears rolling down her face, and said, "But I didn't like it! Why should I lie?"

And her mother had sighed. "Because it's what we do, to be nice."

Anna had decided, at that moment, that *honest* was more important than *nice* when it came to purple polka dots.

She'd been fighting the world ever since.

"At least there are no sharpened, poisoned sticks or a hungry tiger at the bottom," Javi said. "What was that movie where that happened?"

"A gazillion movies," Anna said. "That's not the point. Somebody *dug* this."

"It could have been a robot," Molly said.

"Um, I'm in a hole?" Yoshi called from below.

"I think Anna's right," Javi said, sounding excited. "It feels like . . . a human thing to do."

"Are we going to discuss this for the next month, or are you going to get me out of here?" Yoshi demanded.

Anna heard the noise of stamping. Roars. Like a small stampede.

She quickly dropped the antigravity device into Yoshi's waiting hands.

A group of kids rounded the path, running full tilt and brandishing makeshift spears made out of sharpened sticks. They wore tattered clothes interwoven with reeds and plants. They were running so fast that they came within several feet of the Killbots before slamming to a halt.

The two groups looked at each other, stunned.

Anna felt her stomach lurch. Suddenly, the air felt thick and spongy, as if she could leave fingerprints on it. And then they were in the air.

Yoshi

Yoshi rose from the pit, his katana held in attack position. He didn't know what the noises were, but he wasn't taking any chances. He liked to meet uncertainty with a sharp sword.

He wasn't expecting to see a crowd of other kids spinning in the air, grabbing on to each other's elbows and ankles in a stunned, frantic effort to stay grounded to *something*. They looked like really dumb astronauts practicing for a spacewalk.

It was the first time he'd felt like laughing since they'd crashed.

But that would be wrong, right?

Unfair, too. Anna and Javi had found the first antigravity device near the crash. He knew from experience that the first time you found yourself floating in low gravity, it wasn't easy.

It had taken a while for the Killbots to figure out how to control the devices and how to control themselves in the air when low grav hit. They used bungee cords to keep themselves together, and they'd pretty much mastered the art of leaping into the air and keeping to a general direction as they floated back down.

Molly and Javi had navigated their way to the low branch of a tree. Anna, Kira, and Akiko had grabbed on to a tall bush with spear-like leaves. Yoshi used the momentum of his leap to drift over solid ground.

"Turn it off, Yoshi!" Molly yelled.

Even though Yoshi resented being given orders, he felt it was a good idea to obey this one. He clicked the device to restore normal gravity.

Everyone crashed to the ground, and he heard a few yeows and yelps. There was one high female voice that cried, "Jeepers!"

"You could have warned them," Molly muttered, picking herself up.

"Could have," Yoshi said. "Didn't."

A tall, wiry boy stepped forward. He glowered at them and brandished what Yoshi first thought was a metal pipe. Looking closer, he saw it was a musical instrument.

"Who are you? Where did you come from?" the boy asked, shaking it at them.

"Dude, chill," Anna said. "You're going to threaten us with an *oboe*?"

"They speak English!" A blond girl with braids tied off with vine tendrils bounced in happiness.

"Wonderful," Kira said in Japanese. "They speak English."

The blond girl with braids looked over at her, then at Yoshi. "At least some of you. Are you . . . Americans?"

"Um, mostly," Javi said, "And we're super happy to see you. That pit of danger was pretty awesome, by the way."

"We needed a warning system," the boy with the hard gaze said. He glanced into the woods. "This place is full of creatures you don't want to meet. Anyway, who *are* you? Why are you here?"

"Probably the same reason you're here," Molly said. "Our plane—"

"Crashed," he interrupted impatiently. "Obviously. Where did you come from?"

"New York—"

"No," he said scornfully, "not where are you from, where did you *crash*? Is it far? Can we salvage materials?"

"We took what we—"

"Do you have a shelter?"

"Why do you get to ask the questions?" Molly asked, her chin lifted in that way that meant she was about to go all alpha on him. "Who are *you*?"

The blond girl answered. "We're the Cub-Tones, from Bear Claw, Oregon!" she said. "Boy oh boy are we glad to see you! Our plane crashed, too!"

That was too much enthusiasm for Yoshi. He gave Molly the device, took out his cloth, and began to wipe his katana. It wasn't as though he wanted to scare them or anything. He always wiped down his sword before he sheathed it again. If they were intimidated in the process, that was just a bonus.

The girl leaned in to whisper to Molly. "Is he one of those Japanese soldiers from the war who doesn't know it's over?"

"What?" Anna asked. "What war?"

"Does he speak English?" the girl persisted. "Is he . . . friendly?"

"I'm friendly," Yoshi said in a cool tone. "My sword, not so much. And I'm not a soldier; I'm a student. I live in Brooklyn Heights."

"Like in *The Patty Duke Show*?" she squealed. "Identical cousins!"

Yoshi looked at her blankly. "Identical *cousins*? That's idiotic."

"Jeepers, I miss TV," the girl said, sighing.

"What are they saying?" Kira asked Yoshi in Japanese. "I can't understand."

"I'm not sure I understand, either," Yoshi answered. "And I speak English."

"Hey, we're off track here," Molly said. "Are you the only survivors?"

"Yes." Another girl spoke up. She was petite, with red hair. "And the weird part is, we don't really know what happened. Everybody else just . . . got sucked out. We weren't even hurt."

Yoshi and Molly exchanged a quick glance. The same thing that had happened to them. A blinding pulse of light, and before they could even blink, people, passengers, strangers, the Killbots' faculty adviser, Mr. Keating—they were all just *gone*.

"How long have you been here?" Anna asked.

A chorus of voices spoke at the same time. Each answer was a question.

"Six months?"

"Maybe eight months or something?"

Akiko gave a little gasp. Yoshi knew what she was thinking. Eight months sounded like forever. He couldn't imagine being here that long.

"We lost track," the boy with the oboe said. "I had a watch, but it broke. Time gets funny when every day is the same." He gestured at the device in Molly's hand. "Is that what made us float?"

"It was neato," the blonde said.

"It's something we found," Molly said, putting it back in her pack.

"We found a weird device, too." This was spoken by a girl who hovered behind the blond girl's shoulder. Her voice was soft and trailed away at the end of the sentence, as if she was afraid someone would contradict her.

"Come on, we'll show you the compound," the tall boy

said. "We've been here a long time, so we have shelter and food. You look like you could use it."

"We call it Camp A-Go-Go," a boy with tousled hair said, flashing a friendly grin. He was almost as tall as the wiry boy, but with a thick chest and muscled legs.

"No, *you* call it that," the tall boy said.

"Sounds great, dude," Javi said. "Whatever you call it. We just crossed the blood sand, and it was grim."

"Blood sand?" the muscular boy echoed.

"The red desert."

He nodded. "We tried going that way, but we had to turn back."

"Smart move," Javi said.

"Have you ever seen any sign of rescue planes?" Anna asked as they started down the path.

The wiry boy shook his head. "Not one. Although the sky is almost always hazy with mist and clouds."

"We're in some kind of hidden valley, we think," the blond girl said.

"*Really* hidden," the red-haired girl said.

Yoshi quickly summarized the conversation for Akiko and Kira.

"Just like us," Kira said.

Akiko looked stricken.

"What's the matter, sister?" Kira asked. "There's food ahead. Shelter."

"Don't you see?" Akiko said. "They've been here for . . .

months. So many months, they've lost track. And they're still waiting for rescue. Rescue that isn't coming."

They knew the search had been called off, but Yoshi could tell they all still hoped. They still looked overhead for jet trails. Froze when they thought they might have heard the noise of a jet engine. They had run like fools when they'd heard that music. Stupid fools who still had hope that someone out there would rescue them.

But these kids had been here for months . . . and seen nothing.

Molly

The wiry boy with the oboe was named Hank. He was clearly the leader. Bobby, the burly guy with the cheerful grin, was bigger and stronger, and the kids called him Crash. Molly saw how he deferred to Hank. Dana, the redhead, seemed smart and welcoming. The happy blonde, Kimberly, made a huge mistake when she asked Yoshi to repeat his name three times and then asked if he was "going steady" with Akiko. When Yoshi only glowered, she'd gushed, "Oh, you guys would be so cute together!" Yoshi just snorted and stalked away while Kira giggled.

Stu and Drew were two guys who hung together, and Molly could already tell that she'd have trouble telling them apart. And Pammy, the one with the soft voice, was too shy to say much at all.

The music? They were part of a marching band, the Cub-Tones. State champions!

Standing in the middle of the small compound, Molly had to admire how they'd made a home. It looked as though they'd swept the dirt with branches, for the ground was hard-packed and free of stones and debris. A crudely fenced vegetable plot of some kind was just outside the compound. Sturdy lean-tos surrounded the central fire pit. They were built next to each other except for a larger one at the very edge of the clearing. Unlike the others, which had woven vines arrayed as a kind of curtain, the far shelter had an actual door, made out of sticks. Storage, Hank said.

A fire burned briskly in a pit, with a pile of stacked wood a few yards away. The fire was surrounded by cubes that were oddly translucent and glowed with a blue light.

Hank picked up one of the blue cubes. "This is what saved us," he said. "It's water."

"No way," Javi said in disbelief.

Hank fished in his pocket and brought out a doughnut-shaped metal ring, similar to their device. "See? It's like yours, I think."

Molly took the ring out of her pocket and put it on the table next to Hank's. "Not *like* ours. They're identical."

"So, wait . . . these can mess with gravity?"

She nodded. "Turns it down and turns it up, basically. It also has a setting that messes with technology, but it's less predictable."

"Where did you find yours?" Anna asked.

"Deep in the woods when we were trying to get to the ridge," Hank answered. "We discovered a different setting completely by accident."

He poured water from a pitcher marked *Trans World Airlines* into a rectangular container. Then, holding the ring close to the water, he twisted it so that a set of symbols on the outer and inner rings lined up.

Yoshi recognized those symbols. It was a combination they had yet to try on their own ring.

A blue light began to pulse on the device, and the water in the container slowly thickened. Soon the water was a translucent cube.

Hank upended the container and handed the cube to Javi. "We call it the water-changer."

"It's so light," Javi said, hefting it. "Wow. We *really* could have used this in the desert." He handed it to Molly, and the Killbots passed it along from one to the other.

"It's how we carry water back here from the stream," Dana informed them.

"But the ones by the fire look like they're glowing," Molly pointed out.

"Exactamundo," Crash said. "That's what makes this device such a gas."

"It's a gas?" Anna asked. "Fascinating."

"Not literally," Hank said. "Watch."

Hank took back the cube and held the device close to it. He

twisted the ring and touched a different symbol. A red light began to blink. They all jumped when a jagged line suddenly moved like a bolt of lightning through the gel. Now it glowed with blue light. Hank handed it to Molly.

"It's warm," she said.

He nodded. "We leave them by the fire at night, and they throw off heat."

"These rings are capable of so much more than we realized," she said. "Amazing."

"How do you change it back into water?" Yoshi asked.

Hank pressed the symbol down again. The gel cube was soon a puddle of water on the table.

"Crazy, right?" Crash grinned.

"We wouldn't have made it without the device," Dana said. "The fire pit stays warm longer at night—we think the gel cubes keep it at a constant temperature. Plus, the light keeps the animals away. Saved our lives. That and the tubers."

"Tubers?" Molly asked.

"Tubers are like potatoes?"

"I know," Molly said patiently. "You found them growing here?"

Dana nodded. "We discovered them growing wild. All the plane food ran out pretty quickly, so we were lucky to find something edible."

Yoshi squatted to examine the gel cubes. "This material is like the map we saw in the cavern," he told Molly. "It's like an aerogel."

"Aerogel," Hank repeated. "That's a good name for it. Wait, did you just say you saw a map of where we are?"

Yoshi nodded. "It was in a cliffside cavern. The map showed that we're in a really narrow valley—a rift. At the far end is something that looks like a tower, or a building."

"But who made the map?" Kimberly asked.

"We don't know."

"We guess whoever brought us here," Molly said.

The Cub-Tones gathered closer. "A building?" Dana asked, her green eyes wide. "You mean, with people in it?"

"We don't know that, either," Molly said. "We just figure that there are answers there. Maybe help. That's where we're headed." Yoshi had described the map in detail to her. It had hung suspended in the air, a soft, moving display of shimmering data that revealed they were in a series of manufactured biomes. The building was ten times as big as a plane. It had a pulsing red core. That meant activity, maybe life.

"Have you tried hiking out of the forest?" Javi asked the Cubs. "Not into the desert, but in the other direction?"

"Many times," Hank said. "We can't get to the top of that ridge." He gestured beyond the compound. Through the dense trees, they could barely glimpse the line of the same ridge they'd seen earlier.

"Why not?" Molly asked.

"First of all, the woods are full of predators," Hank answered. "Big jungle cats. A giant bird strong enough to lift a full-grown man."

"I've met both of them," Yoshi said, remembering his encounter with a cougar-like creature. "I think we can handle them."

Hank gave him a look of disbelief. "Yeah," he said. "Easy as pie."

"Plus the jawbugs," Stu said. "They attack every—"

"—night," Drew finished. "But we build up the fire and—"

"—play music," Stu interrupted. "They really hate Mozart."

"But the worst is this huge, terrible beast that looks like an enormous duck," Kimberly said. "I know that sounds funny, but it's not. Its beak is long and sharp, and it's really aggressive."

"We call it—" Stu said.

"—big beak," Drew finished.

"Like Big Bird?" Javi asked. "But if he wanted to kill you instead of teach you the alphabet?"

"Um, what?" Drew asked.

"How would a big bird teach you the alphabet?" Stu added.

"We call it the dreadful duck of doom," Javi said.

"A triple D," Crash said. "Just like my report card!"

"It seems highly intelligent," Hank said. "It knows where we are and even our routines. We think it sleeps in the mornings, so that's when we go for water. It hunts mostly at dusk. There may be more than one, but it's hard to be sure. There's also an animal that looks like a giant hog, but it has a tail like a boa constrictor. We call it the snakehog. If you see it, get out of the open. It's fast. It uses the tail to squeeze the air out of you, and then bites your head off."

The Cub-Tones went silent.

"There used to be a lot more of us," Hank said.

"Poor Dave," Kimberly murmured.

"And Cal," Pammy said.

"That's enough," Hank said. "We don't need to go over it."

Dana put her hand on his shoulder. "You're not still blaming yourself for what happened to Cal—?"

"Not just Cal," Hank said, a hint of sharpness in his tone. "Dave, and Peggy, and Nancy, and Gil."

"We lost people, too," Molly said quietly.

"Well, you may as well get comfortable here," Hank said. "Because going back out there? You'll never get out alive."

6

Javi

Following Hank's warning about the many dangers of the woods, Yoshi gave a great, contemptuous snort and moved away, prowling around the campground.

"Gosh, he's not exactly a people person," Kimberly said.

"He is when you get to know him," Javi said. "Well. When maybe you get to know him *really* well. He'd give you the shirt off his back. He actually *did* give me this shirt." He could tell he was babbling, so he shut up.

And hadn't they mentioned *food*? When people mentioned food, shouldn't they produce it? Javi was relieved when Dana got up and began to set out plates and bowls on a makeshift table. It was just large branches wrapped over and over with vines, braced by what appeared to be airline seats without the upholstery.

Javi's mouth watered and he could barely keep still as

Dana put fruit and some sort of cakes on the table, along with jugs of water. Then she waved them over.

"Eat slowly; you folks look kind of starved," she said.

Javi gulped down the water. It was clear and cool, a far cry from the gritty water they'd been forced to boil in the desert. He could almost feel his body drinking it in.

"Slowly, I said!" Dana repeated. "That goes double for the water."

"Dana's father is a doctor," Kimberly explained. "She takes care of us."

"Sorry," Javi said, wiping his mouth. He took a bun and a piece of fruit, and managed to refrain from shoving both in his mouth at once.

"Where do you get bread?" Molly asked.

"The tubers," Dana explained. "We can grind them into a paste and make buns. A little starchy, but we think they must be full of nutrients, because we stay pretty healthy."

"As long as an animal doesn't get us," Hank growled, reaching for a bun.

"So what's your theory about this place?" Molly asked crisply. "Conjectures?"

Javi bit his lip to hide his smile. Molly was treating the marching band like they were in the robotics club.

"We think maybe there was a Commie spy on the plane," Kimberly said.

Yoshi shifted to face her. He snorted. "Commie?"

"A Russki," Kimberly said, nodding. "And all this"—she

spread her arms—"this weird place is like a giant experiment. And it got out of control, and they abandoned it."

"Because where else are you going to build a secret pinko fake world but Nowheresville?" Crash asked.

"So you think the Soviets made all this?" Molly asked, skepticism in her voice.

"Of course," Kimberly answered. "It's the only explanation, really."

"Not the *only* one," Anna said.

"There are always multiple answers," Molly chimed in. "The trick is to approach each hypothesis and test it."

"So what's your explanation?" Hank asked.

"We haven't been able to test our hypotheses," Molly said, avoiding the question. Javi knew what she was trying not to say. She didn't want to tell them about the metal pod they'd found in a pond. How they were certain that some kind of creature was inside. Maybe the same creature he'd seen in skeletal form out in the desert—angular and hideous but more like a human than an animal.

A creature alien and horrible. *Akumu.* Japanese for "nightmare."

They didn't have to tell the Cub-Tones everything at once. There was enough bad news to go around.

"We haven't been here very long," Javi said. "We know we're on Earth because we saw the stars, and that's about it."

"You mean you thought we might be on Mars?" Crash shook his head, laughing. "I haven't seen any little green men around."

"Well, we agree that this place seems to be manufactured," Molly went on. "We just don't know by who. Whoever created it made it deadly. So why were we saved in the first place?"

"None of the animals quite look like they're supposed to," Dana said. "We think it might be radiation exposure."

"From what?" Molly asked.

"A-bomb testing," she answered. "Maybe this was a restricted area where Russia tested the Bomb."

"The mutations would take generations," Anna pointed out. "Longer than atomic bombs have been around."

"And I'm not sure that explains enough of the weirdness," Molly said.

Javi could tell that none of the Cubs believed her. They had their own crazy theories. But they were in a crazy world, so who was he to argue?

"Why were you all on the plane together?" Javi asked.

"We were at the Macy's Thanksgiving Day Parade and flying home," Hank explained. "There was a storm, and we got routed farther north."

"The parade was a blast," Kimberly said. "I met Lorne Greene! Ben Cartwright! I got goose bumps, even though he isn't crushworthy like Little Joe."

Javi frowned. Almost every time Kimberly opened her mouth, she said something he didn't understand. Oregon sure was a long way from Brooklyn.

Akiko pointed to her own flute and said carefully, "I play, too."

"That's neat," Kimberly said. "I play the piccolo and guitar, but I didn't bring my guitar. We ... should ... play ... together." She spoke slowly and carefully, and Akiko rolled her eyes at Kira.

"Plus, I'm a cheerleader," Kimberly added.

"Of course you are," Yoshi muttered.

"Hank plays the oboe, and I'm *our* flutist," Dana said. "Pammy is trumpet, Stu is French horn, and Drew is saxophone. Crash plays the cymbals and the glockenspiel."

Javi laughed. When the Cubs turned to him, he said, "Sorry. It's just a funny word."

"It's not easy to play, dad," Crash said. "You think because I'm a football player I can't play the glockenspiel?" He cocked his head and frowned. Javi had a sudden uncomfortable flash to Derrick Verlanski making him hand over his math homework in third grade.

"No worries, dude," Javi said. "I'm sure you rock."

"I rock around the clock," Crash said, and did a little twist. "Cooler than Bobby Darin in a snowstorm."

"We were in New York City for two whole nights," Kimberly said. "It was a gas. We had dinner right in Times Square at the Howard Johnson."

"Who?" Javi asked.

"I wanted to sneak into the Peppermint Lounge, but Kimberly was a drip," Dana said, nudging Kimberly with a smile.

"My mom would kill me if I went to a discotheque!" Kimberly squealed. "Besides, we never would have gotten in. But I practiced the twist in our hotel room," she added, doing a little twisting step next to Crash. "I wanted to hear Joey Dee and the Starliters. They are just dreamy. If I lived in New York, I'd sneak in for sure."

Javi watched Kimberly plant one foot and twist her hips. Something was weird. Very, very weird.

"The Beatles went there last year after they performed for Ed Sullivan!" Kimberly continued. "And when Jackie was in the White House, she put in a mock Peppermint Lounge for a party. It's practically historic, you know?"

Jackie *Kennedy*? The Killbots exchanged worried glances. Had Kimberly been here too long? Had she lost her mind? The other Cubs didn't seem alarmed.

"Um, how long has the Peppermint Lounge been open?" Molly asked. "I always forget."

"It's still popular!" Kimberly exclaimed defensively. "Because of the song, the 'Peppermint Twist,' remember? My older sister had the record, 1961."

"Which means your plane went down . . ."

"November 1965," Kimberly said. "We told you."

Javi exchanged an incredulous glance with Molly. "But—" he started, but Molly stepped hard on his foot. Why was Molly picking on him? Anna was the one with no filter. She blurted out the truth at the worst moments. Where had she gone, anyway? She had to hear this. Javi scanned the campground. Anna was nowhere in sight.

"We're guessing it must be 1966 by now, right?" Dana said. "Time goes fast, I guess."

"Yeah," Javi said. "Supersonic fast."

Yoshi repeated the date in Japanese to Akiko and Kira. Their eyes went wide.

How could they tell these kids that they'd actually been here for over fifty years?

And they were exactly the same age as when they'd arrived.

Hank looked around the campground. "Hey," he said. "What happened to Anna?"

7

Anna

Anna followed the flying insect just a few steps into the woods. She'd never seen such an unusual insect. The iridescence of the wings was off the charts—a mixture of aqua blue and deep green and a shock of orange. It looked like a praying mantis, but the head was so large it was hard to believe it could fly with such accuracy and speed.

She had to get a closer look.

The insect flitted from one branch to another. Here the trees were spaced widely enough that she could easily follow. She wished that Kira were with her to draw it. If she ever got out of here—*when* she got out of here—she wanted to have a whole book of drawings and descriptions of what they'd seen. She'd started out here as a robotics nerd, but she was coming back a biologist.

Or, considering what they suspected, some sort of astro-biologist.

The insect flew on, and she ran after it. Anna had always been interested in science. It was her best subject in school, and she constantly read science books at home. Her mother was a nurse who wished she'd become a doctor. Her father was a contractor who had wanted to be an architect.

Anna wasn't going to compromise. Ever.

She darted through the forest after the insect. It zoomed upward and she lost it in the blur of green and blue. She turned around. Then around again. She didn't feel dizzy, or disoriented. She felt completely clear. Yet she had lost sight of the compound, and worse than that, she wasn't quite sure how to get back.

She couldn't discern one blade of grass that had been flattened, one footprint in the soft dirt. She couldn't see the high ridge in order to orient herself. It had been just there on her left when she'd started.

She walked in one direction, but nothing looked familiar. She turned and walked a different way. Then another. She felt her breath beginning to shorten, sweat springing up on her hairline.

She couldn't panic. Panic didn't help the lost. She looked around for a tree to climb, and noticed for the first time that the branches started high up on the trunks, too high for her to reach.

Some of the trees had dropped enormous, stiff cones. She

gathered twelve of them and placed them in a circle. She placed a stick on top of a cone, marking the twelve o'clock position.

She walked forward for a hundred yards, looking for the ridge. Not this way, she was sure of it. She went back and moved the stick to the one o'clock position. She struck out again in that direction, walking another hundred yards or so before turning around.

Slowly, she made her way around the circle. Nothing looked familiar.

She was still lost.

She'd only been walking for maybe . . . ten minutes? The compound couldn't be far. Probably she should just remain right here and wait.

Someone would find her.

She tried not to think about when dusk would fall. Triple D hunting time. Big cats. A bird that could pick up a person.

To keep her mind off her fear, she examined the woods around her more closely. Something was nagging at her. There was something off about this environment. She didn't recognize the species of the trees or bushes, but that was the new normal, so that didn't bother her. Something else did, but she couldn't figure out what it was.

Maybe it was why she'd chased the mantis in the first place. It was sort of hyper-real, with that big head and bulging eyes. Now she was in a grove full of unfamiliar trees. Their trunks were massive, each as big as a small car, but then they narrowed above her head, then widened again. The leaves were different colors at different levels, blue and green.

She watched as a yellow flower bloomed before her eyes, then drooped, dried, and fell. She stooped to pick it up and examine it. She wished she could enjoy the difference and variety here. She wished she could shake her uneasy feeling.

A rustling in the underbrush to the right of her sent her shooting to her feet.

"Hello?" she called. "Yoshi?"

A pair of yellow eyes stared at her. Blinked.

Not Yoshi.

It has a tail like a boa constrictor . . . It uses the tail to squeeze the air out of you, and then bites . . .

Slowly, she took a step backward. Then another.

"Okay," Anna murmured to herself. "I've got this."

If you see it, get out of the open.

She was in a clearing.

She heard a growl that sent a jolt of panic through her. She had to pick a direction. She walked slowly through the trees, trying not to hurry. The creature stayed hidden, but she could hear it following. She stayed in the thickest part of the woods, squeezing past the trunks of the massive trees. The creature would need space to make a charge.

Alongside the trail, a thicket of bushes grew almost to the first branches of the trees. They were covered in brambles, but so thick and dense that there was no way the creature could attack her if she forced her way through.

Anna pushed into the bushes, ignoring the burrs snagging at her clothes. But the creature didn't stop, crashing through behind her. She tried to move faster as the thorns pricked her skin. Suddenly, she was stepping out the other side of the thicket and found herself totally exposed at the edge of a large clearing.

The animal was behind her. She couldn't retreat. Anna tried to swallow against the dryness in her mouth.

She saw a flash of blue-green. The insect, buzzing toward the edge of the clearing, where a grouping of dead, uprooted trees lay tangled. It was like they'd been heaved up in a violent storm. The insect disappeared into the labyrinth.

Thanks for nothing, little guy. It's your fault I'm in this mess.

Anna looked at the trees again. They were a bleached gray color, barkless, and lay piled upside down. Their branches reached into the earth, and their roots strained upward like grasping fingers. Now that she had a second look, she realized they were alive. They were growing upside down!

And the tangled roots would provide great cover. Could she make it?

The animal was close. So close she'd swear she could smell its breath.

It smelled like blood.

Yoshi

How long had Anna been gone? Yoshi wasn't sure. He just knew he was the best person to track her. He'd taken off without waiting for the others. Yoshi had a bad feeling about this. It wasn't like Anna to wander off alone.

It was more like *him*, actually. And now he was . . . well, not lost, exactly, but not quite sure where he was or how long he'd been here. He'd thought that he could just activate the anti-gravity device and float above the trees for a view. He'd pocketed it when everyone was concentrating on Hank's device. But the canopy was too thick here; getting above it would afford a view of only more leaves.

Okay, he was lost.

Ever since he'd read the letter from his mother to his dad, he'd felt himself becoming a different person. He'd found his suitcase, thrown miles from the crash, and in it the letter he was supposed to deliver but not read. He figured if your plane crashed you got a break on the ethics of reading someone else's mail.

He hadn't realized she'd wanted to get rid of him. Sure, he'd been a pain. He felt split between two worlds, Japan and New York, and two people, a mother who worked sixty-hour weeks and a dad who didn't like him.

Half-American, half-Japanese. Part of half a family.

He didn't think moms gave up on their own kids, though. *You take him. I don't want him.* Well, she didn't say that exactly. She said things in therapy-speak, like, *He needs to figure out who he really is* and *His journey to developing his own identity depends on a more constructive relationship with his father.*

He could imagine his father's reaction if he'd ever had a chance to read that letter. His gaze would have gone flat, and he would have crumpled the paper and tossed it. His father had always been contemptuous of his mother's emotion. Why they'd ever gotten married was a mystery.

Ever since Yoshi had read the letter, he felt himself becoming harder. He was already an outsider to the tightly knit Killbots. He was just a *hafu* with a secret priceless sword in the cargo belly of the plane. He'd smuggled it out of Japan the last time he'd visited his father—well, it was his, after all. His father had clearly said he would inherit the katana. But his father *hadn't* mentioned that it was a national treasure and should never leave the country.

So really, it was *his* fault that Yoshi was on that plane,

smuggling a sword back into Japan. Add it to the list of every-thing his father had to control. He'd turned his son into some kind of corporate ninja.

It was better, really, to accept that you were alone. Maybe a part of him had wanted to join the Killbots, to be a member of their little team. That part was gone. He was only inter-ested in staying alive and getting to the end of whatever this was. He had a goal, and he was going to reach it.

He was tired of hearing *opinions*. Go this way or go that way. "Theories?" Molly would ask, and everyone would have a different one. It just slowed them down.

Inside, Yoshi was a ticking clock. He knew that the longer they were here, the more likely it was they would die.

He was furious with Anna for going off, but he would find her. He had last seen her on the edge of the compound, far from the fire and the lean-tos. She'd been staring into the woods, then up in the air. As if she'd been watching a bird. The next time he'd looked over, she was gone.

He didn't know how he'd lost the path, but he had. It had just . . . disappeared. Now he was moving through thick trees and bushes.

At first he had moved in micro-steps, his eyes darting into the underbrush. He'd found a long blond hair snagged on a leaf. He plunged farther into the woods.

There was no trace of footprints or any indication that Anna had gone this way, so Yoshi used instinct instead. Anna was careful. When she led the way on a trail she didn't just push her way through, she examined her environment. Yoshi tried to think like Anna, move like Anna.

As he made his way through the woods, he realized that he'd been watching her more lately. He liked her company. She didn't get on his nerves. Much. She didn't sugarcoat *anything*. Unlike his mom, who hadn't been straight with him.

He came to a small clearing and stopped. At his feet was a circle of tree cones. Anna had done this, he was sure of it, but why? The last one had been dropped carelessly, as if the person was impatient, or annoyed.

Then he noticed a flattened area inside a bush. He put his hand on the vegetation. Warm. An animal had lain here. Maybe observing Anna as she laid the cones down. Maybe for quite a while. His heartbeat sped up as he remembered the beasts that the Cub-Tones had described.

If Anna was being stalked—assuming she even realized it—what would she do?

Avoid open areas. Take the narrowest route through the trees.

Yoshi squeezed between two adjacent trunks. These trees were different, strange. The trunks wide and then narrow above, then wide again. He made his way quickly but carefully, always choosing the tightest and most difficult path. Once he found a few threads of a T-shirt on a bramble bush. Good. He was going the right way.

He kept on moving, faster now that he knew he was on the right track. He heard snuffling and pushed through the last of the scrub. Yoshi found himself in a wide clearing—standing face-to-face with a yellow-eyed beast with saliva dripping from long, brown teeth.

Not good. The beast snorted out of a piglike nose, the exhalation steaming in the cool air.

"Yoshi!" Anna screamed. "Watch out!"

"You *think*?" Yoshi saw Anna across the clearing, hiding in a thicket of upturned trees, their roots reaching up as if trying to grab the sky. "Are you hurt?"

"No. It won't come in the thicket. It's going to charge! Run!"

He wouldn't have a chance. Yoshi couldn't get by this thing. He drew his katana.

"No, Yoshi, don't, it's too strong!"

The beast charged. He watched the bunch of its muscles, its foaming, dripping mouth, the deathly intent in its eyes. Yoshi seemed to have all the time in the world. He thought Anna was screaming, but he couldn't hear her; his blood was rushing in his ears, and he held his sword easily, lightly.

At the last moment he stepped just a few inches to the side. The beast came close enough that he smelled its rancid breath. In one stroke he came down right behind the neck.

It all happened fast. The beast twisted, snarling. It was quicker than he'd anticipated, given its size. The blow was a glancing one, and its skin was as tough as armor. Yoshi's blade skittered off the hide and clanged against the ground, hitting a rock under the dirt. The impact shuddered up his arm.

The blow had momentarily stunned the beast, but Yoshi

saw he didn't have enough room for a lethal strike. Tactical retreat, then. He dashed toward the trees. He'd make a stand there.

He saw Anna's wide, terrified eyes as he dashed toward her, the run of his life. When he was almost at the stand of trees he saw her mouth open in a shout and he felt the thunder of the hooves behind him.

No time to turn. He jumped.

The heat of the beast fueled his leap. He could feel the full force of ferocity behind him. Yoshi turned sideways to push himself through the trees, and the beast rammed into the trunk, its foaming mouth digging into the bare wood in frustration.

Yoshi had one moment only. He could see the heaving side of the animal, and he drove his sword in with all the strength of his body behind it.

The animal's eyes rolled back, and for one instant, Yoshi saw into its rage and terror. Then it backed up and fell on its side.

Yoshi crashed to his knees.

"Yoshi?"

"I'm okay."

"That was awesome."

Yoshi dragged himself to his feet. He wiped his katana, taking his time, hoping Anna couldn't see his shaking hands. "It's dead."

"I'll say."

"These are weird trees."

Anna regarded the trees. "Weird trees for a weird place. I think they grow upside down. Look at those hexagonal shapes right near the ground. Except they're not quite six-sided. They're sort of . . . warped. I think it's a wasp hive, but it's funny that wasps would build their hive so low here." She looked across the clearing. "Do you know the way back?"

"I think so," Yoshi said. "I came from over there."

She looked at him, puzzled. "No, you came from over there." She pointed in the opposite direction.

"Look where the ground is trampled," he said. "And I crashed through those bushes over . . . " He stopped. Anna was right. The bushes all looked the same now.

"Do you mean you came to find me and you got lost, too?"

"I didn't say that," Yoshi said irritably. "I'm not lost."

He gazed out at the clearing. Nothing looked familiar.

"I don't know which way to go," he admitted. He kicked the tree in frustration, then ducked as a large mantis-like insect flew toward him.

"Watch out!" Anna saw the mantis buzz higher. "You don't want to disturb the hive. They might sting. They're like bumblebees—aerodynamically, they shouldn't be able to fly. But look how fast that guy is."

"There's another one," Yoshi said.

And then another, and another. The bugs seemed to come from nowhere, rising up, darting toward them as if taunting them, then flying above their heads. Soon a cloud of them had gathered.

"Um . . . " Anna said, waving the air. "OW!"

One of the mantis bugs had chomped on her arm. Yoshi waved another away from his face. It circled around and buzzed by his ear. A quick, electric pain pulsed.

"I think these are the insects they call jawbugs," Yoshi said.

Five, ten, twenty more flew into the cloud. Yoshi could hear the buzz of wings and jaws working.

Clack clack clack clack.

"Fight or flight?" Anna whispered.

There was a time to make a stand. There was a time to run.

The punishing voice in his head that was his father said, *Cowards run, brave men stand.*

Dad, I'm starting to realize something. I'm smarter than you.

"Run," Yoshi said.

Molly

The light was lowering. Shadows were blue pools under the trees. Hank and Kimberly led the way. They'd left the rest of the Cubs at the compound, but all the Killbots had joined them on the search. Two of their own were out there.

Yoshi and Anna had now been gone for hours.

Hank and Kimberly had explained that they were moving in a spiral around the compound, gradually widening out. It was the only way to navigate. They would get lost if they tried to go straight. They dropped blue light cubes to mark their path as they went and carried makeshift bows and arrows: "Not that accurate, but better than nothing," Kimberly said with a shrug.

"But how do you know which way to go?" Molly asked. "I'm already confused."

"We have one marker," Kimberly explained. "See that rust-colored moss?" She pointed at a tree nearby. A creeping red growth, barely distinguishable from the bark, inched up the tree. "Moss grows on the north side of trees back home. For some reason, this moss always faces the compound. It's hard to spot, and we still get lost all the time. But if we can find that moss, we know where the compound is."

"If we're out here at twilight, we're going to be in trouble," Hank said. "The light cubes don't stay lit for very long if they're not picking up energy from the fire."

"Have you figured out how to track the moon phases?" Molly asked.

"No, the mist is always too thick," Hank said. "Sometimes it will take on a tinge, or clear for a few minutes, and we can see. But not often. We've noticed that the green moon means the animals are more likely to attack, though."

"We call it *midori*," Javi said. "That's *green* in Japanese."

"Neato," Kimberly said. "I like it. And watch out for a green vine that moves. We call it *creeper*. It will twine around you and pull you down."

Javi nodded. "We call it *tanglevine*."

"That's good!" Kimberly approved. "Shucks, you guys are so much better at naming things!"

"There's a clearing just ahead," Hank said. "We should have a lookout for snakehogs."

"I don't think we have to worry about that one," Molly said.

In front of them, the body of an animal was lying on its side, almost wedged between a grove of strange trees, their roots rising in the air. A pool of blood seeped into the dirt.

"A snakehog," Kimberly said. "Wow. They're impossible to kill."

Way to go, Yoshi.

"I think I just became a vegan," Javi said.

"What's that mean?" Kimberly asked.

"It's sort of like a vegetarian, only even more annoying," Javi answered, looking anywhere but at the snakehog.

Hank crouched by the animal. "They must be close. This happened not too long ago."

Molly lifted her head. Lately, her sense of smell had intensified. Sometimes this wasn't so great, but right now . . . she could smell the creature, which turned her stomach over. There was something else, too, though . . . something fresh, something blue. "Is there water nearby?"

"A stream," Kimberly said. "It . . . changes direction, somehow? We never know when we'll be able to find it. That's why having the gel water is so important."

"It's close," Molly said. "If I were lost, I might follow a stream."

"I'd follow GPS," Javi said, looking around.

"Follow what?" Kimberly asked.

"Um, it's short for 'good positioning skills,'" Molly said, lifting an eyebrow at Javi.

"Following that stream will just get them more lost," Hank

said. He looked over and spoke sharply to Javi. "Don't go into that grove."

Javi paused, his hand inches away from a tree trunk. "Why? I want to see the trees."

"Jawbugs nest in there," Hank said. "It won't be pretty."

"Well, the *bugs* are pretty," Kimberly said. "But gosh, do they bite."

Molly pointed to the trees and shook her head at Akiko and Kira. *"Abunai,"* she said.

"Dangerous," Javi explained to the others as a jawbug appeared over his shoulder.

"Move away from the trees," Hank said quietly. "Slowly. Now."

Javi retreated, taking slow steps.

"Good," Kimberly said. "Where there's one, usually others follow. But I don't see any more of them. They tend to swarm in the evening."

"We'd better get out of here anyway," Hank said.

"Theories?" Molly turned to Javi, Akiko, and Kira. She knew the sisters were learning English at a rapid rate. With any luck, they had an idea.

Akiko pantomimed walking out into the clearing, seeing something alarming, and running for the trees.

Molly nodded. "I think that's what happened, too. One of them, or both of them, were stalked by the snakehog and took cover in the trees. Then—"

"The jawbugs attacked," Kimberly said. "So they probably ran—"

"To the stream," Javi finished. "That's what I'd do."

Molly nodded again and led the way. The smell of water and vegetation grew stronger. Within a few minutes she could hear the rushing sound of the stream. They pushed through some reeds and saw Yoshi and Anna just picking their way to the bank. Molly felt relief course through her, but it came out in a rush of annoyance.

"You idiots!" she shouted.

"Nice to see you, too," Yoshi said.

Now Molly could see that he looked exhausted. Water dripped down his cheeks, making tracks in the mud smeared on his skin. Blood dripped down his neck. Anna examined a cut on her arm. Her cheek had a painful-looking swollen bite.

"I'm sorry, I was just scared," Molly said in a low tone. "We've been searching for you for an hour."

"One hour? Try three," Javi said. "Are you guys okay?"

"I've been better," Yoshi said. "What are those bugs? People-eaters?"

"They chomp pieces out of you," Kimberly agreed.

"I'll say," Anna said, examining her bloody knee. "They chased us and we jumped into the stream. We had to find a place where it was deep enough to go under. Then we sat in the stream until they went away." Her teeth chattered. "I'm freezing."

"We've got to make tracks," Hank said tersely. "The dark is gathering. It's prime hunting time for the big beak."

"Not to mention the Thing," Kimberly said.

"The Thing?" Anna asked. "You didn't say anything about a Thing."

"We've never actually seen it," Kimberly said as they quickly moved through the forest, aiming for the faint blue glow of the light cube ahead. She picked it up and put it in her pocket. "We hear it."

"It's big enough to shake the ground," Hank said. "We don't want to run into it."

The blue lights of the cubes ahead were starting to flicker and dim. The chilly night wind—what the Killbots called *yokaze* thanks to Akiko and Kira—was making Yoshi and Anna shiver.

Hank moved quickly, setting the pace, occasionally giving a worried glance at the sky. There was no sun, just a gradual dimming of light that meant evening was coming on fast.

Anna stopped suddenly. A small, moving green cloud was ahead, blocking their way. "Jawbugs," she said. The trauma of the recent attack made her go pale.

"Will they attack?" Molly asked.

Hank kept a wary eye on the cloud. "They only attack in large numbers. Maybe we'll get lucky."

A few more bugs joined the cloud.

"Let's keep moving," Hank said. "Everybody hold a light cube. It will help a little. They're not afraid of it, exactly, but they don't like it."

They walked, watching as more and more jawbugs joined the cloud. A tight group of the insects broke off and swooped down at Javi, brushing against his forearm as he protected his eyes. One of them bit. "Ow!" he shouted, waving the light cube.

The cloud wheeled and swooped down, attacking Hank. He covered his face and darted and weaved, trying to avoid them. The bugs attacked again, diving and snatching at their clothes, moving so fast they were a blur, terrifying and relentless.

"Everybody hold a cube over your head!" Molly called.

Kimberly quickly passed cubes among the group. As soon as they each held one, Molly barked another order.

"Now run!" she yelled.

Molly held her cube high over her head and burst forward, followed quickly by Javi, Anna, and the others. The cubes cast their strange light through the forest, giving the woods an eerie, fairy-tale quality.

The insects hovered just above, jaws working, wings fluttering. Molly heard a jagged buzzing noise as one swooped close to her ear, then she felt a shock of pain. She bludgeoned the jawbug with her cube, sending it spiraling away, but the electric sting of the bite still burned.

What would it feel like to be stung by a whole cloud of those things?

Behind her, Kira yelped, *"Itai!"* Molly could only guess that meant *ouch.*

"These lights will fade soon," Hank huffed. "We have to get back to the compound. Hurry!"

The bugs kept tracking them, swooping again and again only to be driven away by the lights. Why were they so aggressive?

"This is starting to feel *personal*!" Javi yelled, running and swatting. It was like he'd read Molly's mind.

The fire at the compound was now visible through the trees. They ran for it, finally stumbling past the border. Dana, Stu, Drew, and Pammy leaped to their feet, startled.

"Jawbugs!" Hank shouted. "Get in positions!"

The Cub-Tones moved quickly and assuredly, taking up their instruments. Dana handed Hank his oboe. At a nod from Hank, they began to play.

The music flowed out from the instruments and soared into the air. Hank's oboe took the lead, playing a melody that seemed to twine around the trees and fill the forest. The bugs wheeled away with it, riding the music until they disappeared.

"Uh, wow," Javi said. Akiko clapped joyfully, while Kira peppered Yoshi with questions.

The music stopped, and Dana hurried over to Yoshi with a small jar. "Let me look at you," she said.

"I don't need any help," Yoshi said, twisting away.

"Don't be such a chicken," Dana said. She broke a water cube over a cloth and dampened it. Then she washed away the dirt and blood from his face and dabbed some kind of gel on his cuts. "We experimented with a bunch of plants. This one has antiseptic qualities. It also helps with the pain."

Scowling, Yoshi let her tend to his cuts. "Okay, okay. Now Anna," he said, twisting away.

"What was that, with the music?" Molly asked. "How did you know that would work?"

"The bugs swarm the camp every night," Dana said. "But for some reason, Mozart always drives them away. Clarinet Concerto in A."

Dana turned her attention to Anna, then to the others. Hank was last. He had an ugly cut on his hand. His shirt was shredded. He sat, glowering.

Dana finished and then said gently, "Why don't you keep playing? It might not be too late to capture some whistling birds."

"No, it is too late," he said angrily. "It's almost dark."

"Is that what the net is for?" Javi asked. A net made of densely woven material stretched from one tree to another.

"At dusk we build up the fire," Dana said. "If we play music, it seems to attract these plump little birds. They get too close, and . . . dinner! They taste like chicken."

"We call them slide-whistle birds," Javi said.

"Perfect name," Dana said. "That's exactly what their song is like!"

"They're really good with berry sauce," Javi said.

"We do that, too!" Dana grinned.

"Dinner would be good," Molly admitted. "That was close, out there."

Hank stood. "It wasn't close, it was stupid," he said with sudden fierceness. "This is our compound, our rules. Nobody goes into the woods alone. Ever. And nobody heads into the upside-down trees. They're full of jawbug nests. First you went off by yourself," he said, pointing to Anna, "then you." His furious gaze rested on Yoshi. "The list of things you don't know would choke a snakehog. You endangered all of us. Never be so stupid again."

"Stupid? I'm the one who saved her!" Yoshi said, shooting to his feet.

"Um, you didn't really save me?" Anna said. "I was safe in those upside-down trees."

"You are *never* safe in those trees!" Hank shouted.

"Well, I was," Anna argued. "The hogsnake thing wouldn't enter. Yoshi just went all ninja and disturbed the jawbugs."

Yoshi glowered at Anna, then swiveled back to Hank. "Anyway, you can't give me orders."

"Oh yes, I can," Hank said. "As long as you're here, you obey them. You never leave the compound alone, and you never go into the upside-down tree groves. If you don't agree, we'll take measures to make sure you do."

The tension boiled. Molly saw the deep flush on Yoshi's face. He hated to be cornered, and he hated to be told what to do. Plus, Anna had embarrassed him. Why hadn't she just let him think he'd rescued her?

Hank took a step toward Yoshi. He was older and taller

than Yoshi and all lean muscle. The guy looked intimidating, even holding an oboe. Crash moved to his side, Dana to the other, flanking him. Molly caught a flash of the grit and discipline that had helped these kids stay alive.

Akiko and Kira stood at Yoshi's shoulder, and Javi moved in, too. It was the middle school playground, all over again. Except there was something else here that was deeper and scarier.

"Everybody?" Kimberly spoke up. "Can we cool it, here? It's just silly to argue, considering."

"So now I'm silly *and* stupid?" Yoshi asked.

Kimberly looked from one group to the other. "Oh, golly," she sighed. "I really miss being popular. People used to listen to me, you know? Hank lost his cool, but he's right. He's protected us and he can protect you."

"We don't need his protection," Molly said. She wasn't in the mood to be peacemaker. She was too tired and hungry. Nobody intimidated her crew like this. "We've been doing just fine. At least we push ourselves. At least we're trying to get out of here!"

"Good luck, then," Hank said. He gestured to the dark woods. "There's the door. Have a ball. Go!"

Suddenly, the ground lurched under their feet. Molly stumbled, almost knocking into Hank. The woods came alive with the sound of roaring and screeching.

"It's the Thing," Kimberly whispered.

10

Javi

"You see?" Hank spit out. "The woods aren't safe. Everyone, secure the compound!"

"You've never even seen this 'Thing,'" Yoshi said. "Maybe we should investigate to see what kind of a predator we're dealing with."

"You can hear the animals going crazy trying to get away from it. If you go out there, we'll have to rescue you again. No thanks." Hank turned to Molly. "Control your people. Mine have tasks to do."

Molly and Yoshi both bristled at the order.

"Loser," Yoshi muttered under his breath.

The Cubs moved like a synchronized machine. Stu and Drew threw wood on the fire, building it up. The girls began to place light bricks in a ring around the compound. As soon as Javi figured out what they were doing, he offered to help.

As he hurried to the far edge of the compound, he came close by the lean-to the Cubs called the storage shed. There was a cut-out window in the wood at the back with a flap made of leaves and vines braided together. For a second, he could have sworn the curtain moved.

He thought it must be the night wind stirring it. But then he saw a pale blur, and his heart leaped in his chest with a start of fear.

There was someone in the hut.

When the compound was secure, everyone drew closer to the fire. Gradually, the sound of the animals diminished as the fire burned high.

"Dinnertime in the forest," Anna said. "That's quite a food chain out there."

"And we could have been the main course," Hank said.

Kimberly shot him a warning look. "Hey, Mister Grump, mind your p's and q's. We have new friends around the campfire. We're safe. Let's all get happy, here!"

"As long as you don't make us sing, we're cool," Javi joked.

"And if you don't mind my saying so, you all look as worn out as my old socks," Kimberly added. "You have to stay with us for a few days at least."

"You have a point," Molly admitted. "Traveling across the blood sand took a lot out of us. We need rest."

"You might," Yoshi said. "I don't."

"Yeah," Hank said. "You're Superman. We get it."

"Time to get dinner on the table!" Kimberly sang out.

Javi moved closer to Molly. "I need to talk to you."

"Later," she said in a low tone.

The Cub-Tones moved in what was clearly a familiar rhythm. Drew and Stu served tubers that had been roasting whole in the fire. No slide-whistle birds had been caught, so there was no meat. The tubers, however, were delicious, flaky and hot and just a little bit sweet. Along with them they ate greens that tasted a little too marshy but also a little bit like heaven to the Killbots, who'd been living on very small rations. They all had second helpings. For the first time in a long while, there was plenty to eat and drink.

Dana had also made some kind of tea that filled Javi's belly with warmth.

"My grandmother used to make nettle tea," Dana said. "This is pretty close. Take some more, Javi." She poured more tea into his cup.

Javi leaned back against the log, the china cup warm in his hands. The group's tension had melted away in the relief of firelight and food. It felt so good to have a full belly. Maybe he'd been wrong about something moving in the storage hut. It was easy to mistake a fluttering vine-curtain for something else.

"This is nice," he said, indicating the cup. "You were smarter than we were about salvaging stuff from the plane. China and silver . . . You must have raided the first-class cabin. Our plane blew up, so we weren't able to get much.

Okay, we blew it up. But it was an accident! We found the tech-boosting setting on our device."

Hank looked up. "Tech boosting. You mentioned that before."

Molly pulled the device out of her pack. "You have to be careful with it. It powered up the plane, but the wiring started to spark, and . . . well, boom."

"It's lucky we salvaged everything," Kimberly said. "The woods swallowed up the plane in just a couple of weeks. Most things grow really quickly here. Except for the tubers."

"The tubers were a problem when we first got here," Dana explained. "We found them growing wild, but it was a small patch. They turned out to have a super-long growing season, and we almost starved until Hank figured out how to crop-engineer them." Dana dug into her pocket and slid a small notebook across the table. "He still keeps track of what's planted and when, and crop yields. We always know how much we have and how much is stored."

Anna and Javi both peeked over Molly's shoulder as she paged through the book. Hank had tracked the tuber field from day one and made notations of what was planted and then harvested, counting the tubers by eights and crossing them out with a flourish.

"He sprouted them and then replanted them in a new spot where other vegetation was growing fast," Dana went on. "We think there are spots in the soil that accelerate growth."

"I thought I saw a flower grow and then wither and die in about ten seconds," Molly said, forking in another bite of tuber.

Dana nodded. "That's the hour-flower. They grow and wither superfast."

"It's erratic, but not unheard of," Anna said. "There are insects, like the mayfly, that often live out their whole adult lives in less than a day. Some for just a few minutes."

Dana sighed. "Many of the plants here are like that. The woods are always changing, sometimes overnight."

"Early morning our first chore is to locate the stream," Hank said. "We learned that the hard way."

"Lately it's been getting hard to find," Kimberly told them.

"We stick to that path and don't go deep in the forest at all. You saw what happens when we do," Hank added pointedly.

Yoshi stood. "Bed," he said curtly.

"We're going to double up," Dana said. "You guys can have the two lean-tos close to the fire."

"I don't sleep inside," Yoshi said. He snatched a blanket from a pile and crossed to the other side of the fire.

Akiko, Kira, and Anna squeezed into one lean-to and Molly and Javi took the other. Javi lay down on a pallet of fragrant leaves. The temperature was dropping, and the mist was dense and thick. He was glad of the blanket. It was heavier than the flimsy blankets he remembered on the plane, just like the forks they'd used to eat dinner with were like the ones he used at home. He figured that back in the sixties airlines must have actually spent money on making passengers feel comfortable.

Molly frowned down at the battery device, warm in her hand. She slid under her blanket. "So what did you want to tell me?"

"I'm not sure," Javi said. "I mean, I could be wrong. But I thought I saw movement in that storage shed. There's a window on the other side."

"Movement? Like, an animal? Or a person?"

"I couldn't tell. And it was pretty dark, so . . . I'm not sure." Javi yawned. He could barely keep his eyes open. "Is Hank right?" he asked, trying to suppress another yawn. "Is it too dangerous to keep going?"

"Of course not," Molly snapped. Then she sighed. "We'll rest for a day, but then we move on. We have to find that building. They've been here for over *fifty years*, Javi. They're waiting for rescue instead of finding it themselves."

"How do you think it happened?" Javi asked. "They're the same age as us. Some kind of time warp, right?"

"We messed with gravity," she said. "I guess anything is up for grabs, even time."

"Shouldn't we tell them?"

"I don't know," Molly admitted, flipping over on her side and resting her head on her hand. "I don't know what's right. Think about it. We'd basically be telling them that their parents are dead, or at least really old. I'm not in a rush to do that."

Javi could see why. Molly's father's death had broken her heart.

"They seem comfortable just staying put," he said. What he didn't say was, *It's not bad here.* They'd figured out how to keep a constant supply of water and food, they had pretty much figured out predators, and the lean-to was the most comfortable place he'd been in days. It was warm, the blanket was soft, the firelight played on the walls.

The world that the Cub-Tones knew was gone. No one danced the twist anymore. The Beatles broke up. Who was president in 1965 anyway? Javi felt his eyelids droop.

"Moll? What if we're in a time warp right now, and *we* don't know it?" he asked sleepily.

"Then we'd be in big trouble," Molly said, but Javi was already sliding into a dream and couldn't answer.

Molly

Molly woke feeling disoriented.

She sat up, hugging her knees. Was it close to dawn? This unrelenting sky never told them anything. It was either dark or gray. No sunrise, no sunset. She was sick of it.

She hadn't meant to sleep. It had simply dropped over her.

She had nightmares now every night. She dreamed of a dull metal tower with a red pulsing eye.

She had confusing dreams about the plane crash. Except this time, there was one survivor. He seemed to float vertically in something made of water, or like the aerogel bricks.

Sometimes the nightmare changed, and she was the one in the aerogel. She was something soft turning to hard. Flexible shafts with barbs and hooks that nestled underneath her skin.

She felt her shoulder. There was a long, flexible line under her skin. Even in the darkness she could see the green rash spreading along it. Was it . . . cartilage?

Javi breathed softly next to her, deeply asleep.

What is happening to me?

Molly sat up and stared at her hands. They were the same hands. Strong and brown, with a broken fingernail and a cut on her thumb. She was still herself.

There had been a basic unsaid pact between the Killbots ever since they'd realized that no rescue was coming.

Nobody talked about home.

Never, ever mention parents, or family. Never mention new sneakers and thick hoodies to pull on when you're cold. Never mention movies or soccer. And never, ever mention food. Never mention Javi's mother's delicious arepas sprinkled with cinnamon sugar, never mention clean sheets or water from the tap or YouTube on your phone or your mom's special Saturday breakfast.

Never think about a mound of fluffy eggs with strips of toast your mom would place around the plate like the rays of a sun.

Never think about a kiss on top of a head. Never think about a hug.

Never think about an *I love you* in all its casual uses—*Good-bye, love you!* on the way to school; *Sweet dreams, I love you* before bed; even *Sweetie, I love you but you really have to stop crunching on those pretzels right by my ear.*

None. Of. That.

She'd been okay; she'd been as close to fine as she could get, considering getting bitten by a creature with green blood while you marched toward some fate you couldn't see, but recently, just since they'd reached the woods . . . she was remembering too much. And too clearly.

A memory would be so sharp and sweet and clear that it would almost knock her over. It would be like she was *in* the memory and could feel her mother's kiss or how a Honeycrisp apple sprays when you bite into it. She couldn't stop the memories from coming. They were like a fast punch.

If you remembered too well what you left behind—what you'd maybe never get back to—it could just about kill you.

Or make you so afraid that you couldn't go on.

She was wide awake now, hearing Javi's soft, snuffling breathing. When he was asleep and dreaming he sounded like a puppy.

She wanted to wake him up. Sometimes he saw things in such a kind, logical way that took her longer to figure out.

He had asked the right question. *What if we're in a time warp right now, and we don't know it?*

Maybe instead of a day passing, they'd just gone forward a month. A year. Or five. Maybe time was elastic here; maybe it zoomed ahead and snapped back. Maybe it took giant leaps. Maybe the clock just ticked faster.

It was a terrifying thought. The one thing they had never

questioned in this crazy place was *time*. That continued to move in the usual way, or at least they thought so, without batteries for the phones that had survived the crash. Nobody had a watch. They told time by the sky. It still darkened and lightened. Now that she thought about it, though, she wasn't quite sure how many days they'd been here.

She still had a tiny amount of battery left in the phone she'd found in the luggage, and she knew if she turned it on she'd have maybe a few minutes, but she was saving it for . . . she didn't know what. A last-minute distress call?

Molly pushed aside the blanket. The compound was quiet, everyone in that deep sleep before morning. It was a perfect time to investigate what Javi might have seen.

Molly slipped into her shoes. She eased over to the opening and pushed aside the braided reeds. The fire still burned, an eerie but beautiful blue glow around it. She could see the unmoving lump that was Yoshi rolled in a blanket, asleep.

She looked across at the lean-to with the door. "Storage," Hank had said, dismissing it. But Molly hadn't seen any of the Cubs enter it, not when they got medical supplies to treat their wounds or anything they needed for dinner.

Molly crossed the compound by skirting around the edge and keeping close to the trees that ringed the circle. The mist dampened her hair and made everything look blurry and unreal.

It wasn't until she was almost at the lean-to that she realized someone was sitting outside it.

It was Hank. He sat quietly. The firelight glittered on a knife. It was dipped in something red. Something that looked like blood.

12

Yoshi

*I*diot.

  Stupid.

  Silly.

Yoshi turned over on the hard-packed ground. He couldn't get the words out of his head.

Names his father used to call him.

They needed to pack up supplies and get out of here. If the Cubs wanted to stay, fine. Let Hank play his oboe and let another century go by.

But Molly wanted to wait another day.

Cowards! his father's voice said, and for once, Yoshi agreed. He felt time pressing on him, urging him forward. There was something about this place he didn't trust. If it were up to him, he'd be gone by first light.

What if he *could* go it alone?

Maybe that was the secret to success. Slipping from shadow to shadow, silent, part of the forest. Yoshi thought back to the map. How long would it take him to reach the building? Maybe three days? Four? He could get to the building at the end of the valley on his own, he could find out what all this was about, and then he could . . . solve it, somehow.

He pictured himself striding back into the compound, triumphant. He'd say to Hank, *You were afraid of the forest? It wasn't anything at all, dude. Are you ready to be rescued?*

Hank had never made it to the top of the ridge. But Hank wasn't Yoshi. And Hank didn't have a katana.

Would they miss him? He doubted it. Anna hadn't even cared that he'd come looking for her, how he'd rushed off without thinking (okay, now he could admit it, it was stupid). Molly wasn't interested in his opinion, not when it got in the way of her leadership.

He'd been the one to act first, always. He'd been the one to go for water after the crash, to realize how crucial it was. He'd been the one to figure out they had to climb to the top of the cliff, and that's how they'd discovered that the valley was basically a machine. He'd found the place they had to get to, provided them with a plan and a reason to keep going.

Let the others rest.

He needed to move.

Tomorrow.

13

Molly

Molly froze. Across the compound, Javi had just pushed out of the lean-to and was looking around.

Go back in, Javi!

He caught sight of her and ambled forward. Molly frantically waved at him to stay away before Hank spotted them, but he kept on coming. Hank's head was bent over his lap. He hadn't seen them. Yet.

When Javi reached her, she pulled at his arm, drawing him farther into the shadows. "What are you doing?" she whispered.

"You were gone. I was worried."

"Hank has a knife! I think there's blood on it!"

Javi squinted in the gloom. "What's he doing?"

"Guarding the shed, of course!"

"That's not blood on the knife. It's just the light. *Look.*"

Molly squinted. The firelight cast a reddish tinge to the fog that blanketed the compound. She felt foolish. "Oh."

"I'm going to talk to him," Javi said.

"No, he could be dangerous!"

Javi turned. His warm brown eyes were puzzled. "Why do you think so?"

She wasn't sure. Molly pressed her fingers against her shoulder. She could feel the beating of something there, but it wasn't the pulse of blood moving through her veins. For a moment she'd looked at Hank and seen something . . . *other*.

"Okay," she said. "You distract him, and I'll sneak around to the back."

She darted behind a tree as Javi ambled toward Hank.

"Dude!" he called softly. "Don't you ever sleep?"

Molly slid from shadow to shadow. She saw Hank gesture and Javi lean in. As soon as she was out of their sight line, she crept to the back of the lean-to. A lattice of dark leaves hung over the window.

Molly crept closer. She gently lifted the leaf curtain.

She almost leaped back and screamed when she saw a face looking out at her.

A pulsing green line ran like a toxic river down one side of his face. It split into capillaries and disappeared under his T-shirt.

The . . . *creature* pressed his face close against the opening.

"I felt you coming," he said to Molly. "You're just like me."

*　　*　　*

Breathe.

Breathe.

"Molly?" Javi's voice. "Are you okay?"

Molly came back to herself and found she was on her knees. She saw the clumps of dirt between her fingers. She'd fallen, and she didn't remember falling.

She saw Javi's sneakers.

"Moll? You okay? Did you trip?"

Javi's hand.

"Fine." She let him help her up. "I just stumbled, that's all."

What had happened? The boy had spoken to her, and she had stepped into her nightmare. Just as easily as walking from one room to another.

A rush of compressed air in her ears, a dull metal shine of walls around her, a translucent wall and a pulsing red heart, and then a hand reaching out, poking through the wall as it bent and shuddered, and the hand grasped her shoulder and stroked her . . . *feathers.*

"Come on," Javi said. "Everything's cool. I'll show you why Hank has a knife."

"There's someone in the hut."

"I know."

Molly followed Javi around to the front of the hut. The gray sky was lightening. A few birds were twittering.

Hank was bent over something in his lap, a long, stiff dried plant. He was carving it.

"He's almost out of reeds," Javi explained. "For his oboe. The vibration of the reed inside the instrument makes the music. Very cool."

"We brought lots of reeds on the trip," Hank said. "We were afraid one would break in the parade, so we all brought extra. All the woodwinds in the band. I was able to find all the reed cases from the plane. One reed lasts about two weeks if you're lucky, sometimes three if I don't play very much. I kept thinking I'd be able to make new ones, but so far, no luck. I'm down to maybe ten good reeds now."

"I don't know much about music," Molly said.

Hank held up the plant. It was long and spiky at the end. "This is the closest I could get to cane. I know how to take care of reeds; I just never made one." He pushed his long hair out of his eyes. "It's not easy," he admitted. "I can't get the response I need. If I can't play the oboe, we're down to percussion and flute and some brass. It just won't sound the same."

"I guess that's important?" Molly asked. She stirred impatiently. She didn't want to talk about oboes; she wanted to ask about the boy in the hut.

"Music keeps us together," Hank said. "It just . . . keeps us sane, I guess. And it protects us. It lures the birds for food, keeps away jawbugs." He continued to work on the long, stiff plant. "Kimberly has been teaching me the piccolo. I'm not that good at it."

"I get it," Javi said. "Engineering is our music. Figuring out how something works, or how to make something work better, is what we do. I really miss coding for the ROS. Basically a bot is software, the robot is hardware. But the skills are basic, right? See a problem, try stuff, solve the problem."

"I have no idea what you're saying," Hank said.

"Oh right." Javi looked abashed. No doubt he'd just remembered that a computer was the size of a room in Hank's time. "Doesn't matter," he added with his genial grin. "Just engineering stuff. It just means I get it. I think I would have lost it if every day we didn't have something to figure out, or something to fix."

Javi waved in the general direction of the woods. "If you let go of the awful stuff, like the crash and people dying and everything? You've got an engineer's dream out there."

"I see what you mean," Hank said. He lifted a reed out of a small dish of water and fitted it into the oboe.

"Hank's friend Cal played the clarinet," Javi said to Molly.

"The one who died?" Molly asked.

"He didn't die," Hank said. "We never said that. I just changed the subject because . . . " He concentrated on the oboe. "Anyway. He was bitten by a big beak and . . . his mind isn't right."

"He's the one in the hut," Molly said. "You lock him up."

"No! He just gets sort of crazy sometimes. He's the one who likes to stay in there."

Hank blew into his oboe experimentally. A high, almost tuneless sound came out, and he sighed. "Not good."

Suddenly, a bellow came from the hut. "Ratio!"

A shadow passed over Hank's face. "It's Cal. Sometimes he likes the music, sometimes he gets upset."

"Can we meet him?" Javi asked.

Molly hoped Hank would say no. She didn't want to meet Cal. She didn't want to look in his eyes again. The eyes of something not human.

"It's okay," she said quickly. "We don't have to—"

But Hank was already rising and heading to the door. "Come on, then," he said.

14

Javi

Cal sat against the wall. Javi nearly choked. There was a pulsing green line down his cheek like a scar. Smaller lines spread out from it and disappeared under his shirt.

It was the color of Molly's rash. The rash she didn't think he saw.

Cal ignored Javi and stared at Molly. He held up a wristwatch with a cracked face. "Tick-tock, tick-smash," he said.

"My watch," Hank said. "Cal broke it. It was our only way of telling time."

Cal began to drum his fingers on the floor. "Not all sounds operate with the same ratio system."

"Cal, this is Molly and Javi," Hank said. His voice was flat. It was clear to Javi that it was painful for Hank to see his old friend.

"Music, noise, music, noise," Cal said.

Hank shook his head. "Here he goes."

"Four, five, six. Two five six is not the frequency. Chromatic, diatonic, chromatic, diatonic," Cal said.

"What does it mean?" Molly asked.

Hank's mouth twisted. "Nothing. It's just everything in his brain that's all mashed up comes out in pieces. Chromatic and diatonic are scales."

"What does it mean," Cal repeated flatly. It wasn't a question so much as an echo. He leaned forward, his eyes locked on Molly's. "Triple diatonic nonchromatic tempered untempered! Just find the frequency sequence! Maintenance is in damage mode! Intruder!"

"She's not an intruder, Cal," Hank said.

Dana pushed through the door, a mug and plate in her hands. "What are you doing? You're upsetting him!" She turned to Hank accusingly.

Hank held up two hands. "Fine. I'm leaving."

"Don't worry, Cal," Dana said in a soothing voice. "I have your breakfast. Tea. Fruit. See?"

Cal turned to Dana. For one instant only, Javi saw something in Cal's eyes. Something broke through, some sort of human feeling. Cal held out his hand for the tea.

"She's just like me," he said to Dana.

Dana patted his shoulder. "Right." She looked up at the others. "We should go. He's calm when he's alone."

Cal hit the ground hard in an odd rhythm. "Four five six are not the ratios!"

Javi followed Dana out the door.

"Why do you keep him in the hut like that?" he asked her. For some reason, he felt like crying.

"We don't force him!" Dana exclaimed. "But there were a few times when he got kind of . . . violent. He broke Hank's watch. And nearly broke his own clarinet. He basically just tried to rip it to pieces. He was going after my flute when Hank stopped him. It was awful. I don't think Hank has forgiven him for it." Dana hugged herself against the dawn chill. "It's so sad," she said. "He used to be this really smart, fun person. He and Hank grew up together. Best friends since they were little."

"BFFs," Javi said. Then he realized that Dana had no idea what that meant. "Best friends forever," he explained.

"BFF." Dana tried it out. "Yes. Good one. Anyway, the . . . accident happened soon after we got here. Hank and Cal volunteered to go past the stream, try to make it up the ridge. They were gone for weeks. We thought they were dead. They got lost and then they were attacked by what you call the triple D. Hank barely made it back—he had to half carry Cal for miles. Cal ran this horrible fever for days."

Javi nodded. So had Molly. Dread was snaking up his spine.

"Then when he was better, he said he wasn't in pain. The

wound was glowing green, and we just kept putting antiseptic gel from that plant on it. He seemed better. Back to himself. And then, I don't know, he started to change. I can't explain it. At first it was hard to tell. It was little things. It was more like a feeling . . . something was wrong."

"Yeah," Javi said. He swallowed against the lump in his throat.

"Hank really noticed it because they were close. And one day . . . Cal just cracked. He was never the same after that."

Dana shook her head and looked out at the woods. "You know what? We lost good friends here. Dave lived down the street from me. We held hands in third grade. I mean, those deaths were horrible. I saw Dave die." Her chin trembled. "But seeing Cal like this? It's almost worse."

Now Dana was crying, and Javi didn't know what to do. It made him want to cry, too. Over Dana's shoulder, he saw Molly emerge from the hut.

She looked shaken. Lost. She looked past Javi as if he weren't even there.

Anna

There was a place right by her and Kira on the log, flat and dry, but Yoshi took his bun and tea and stood by the fire instead, his back to them. Why did he do that? What was he thinking? It was almost like he was angry at her.

Anna chewed on a bun, made from ground seeds and fruit, which Dana had grilled over the fire. It was flat and chewy, but it wasn't bad. The tea, made from dried nettles and flowers, would have been delicious if only she liked the taste of meadow.

As she ate the seed bun (judging by the chew factor, this could go on all morning), Anna relived the moment when Hank had called her stupid. She wanted to chuck her bun at his head, but that might give him a concussion.

It was a terrible thing to be called stupid. Sometimes people say it if you don't raise your hand in class, or if you prefer sitting alone in the cafeteria. And when you're called stupid, it's easy to begin to think you're stupid somewhere deep inside. Then, no matter how many good grades you rack up in school, you never really feel smart.

Javi was on his third bun and was talking to Stu and Drew. Akiko was playing a melody on her flute while Kimberly joined in on the piccolo. Kira was sketching.

Anna leaned over to watch Kira draw. She never minded if Anna peeked. Kira was sketching the net hung between the trees. It was a detailed drawing, with cross-hatching on the trunks and the leaves rendered delicately.

"Good," Anna said.

"Thanks," Kira said. Then she said something in Japanese. Akiko overheard her and lowered her flute. She frowned, then looked up at the trees.

"Yoshi!" Anna called. "Can you translate?"

Yoshi didn't look happy to be interrupted from staring into space. Kira repeated herself.

"She said things don't quite match here," he said.

"What does she mean?"

A long burst of Japanese from Kira, and Akiko chimed in. They talked excitedly to Yoshi.

Yoshi shrugged. "They don't know."

Anna shook her head. "If you're going to translate, why don't you try actually telling me what they say?"

"I am telling you!"

"No!" Kira blew out an exasperated breath. She pointed her finger at Yoshi. "You're fired."

She reached down and picked up a leaf, then held it against her page. Quickly, she sketched a leaf next to it. Then she stabbed her pencil at it.

Anna leaned closer. She suddenly saw what Kira meant, and what had been bothering her in the woods.

"That's it! That's what I saw, only I didn't realize I saw it! It's asymmetrical! Look at how the blades are attached to the stalk. They aren't opposite each other. And the veins are all over the place. This is . . . very unusual. Symmetry is almost always part of nature's design. Nature prefers thing simple. I wonder . . . "

Anna closed her eyes, trying to remember. Was *that* what had fascinated her about the insect? Were the wing markings, unlike those on a butterfly, asymmetrical?

"The place looked almost normal," she said. "But it violates the laws of nature just as much as our devices. These mutations . . . it's like the living things are carbon-based, but the DNA is twisted in really weird directions."

"Look, everything about this place is screwy, from the moment we landed," Yoshi said impatiently. "If we stopped to try to figure out every bizarre spectacle we see, we'd stay in one place, just like them. We need to leave, now!" He translated what he said to Akiko and Kira. Akiko answered him, and Anna looked to him for a translation.

"She says I'm right," Yoshi said, glaring at Akiko.

"Try again," Anna said. "That wasn't what she said."

Another burst of words from Akiko.

"Okay, okay! She says we don't know what's ahead, but if it's as bad as what's behind us, we'll need to be strong. That's why she agrees with Molly about staying another day. She said . . . what happened to Oliver knocked us down."

Kira nodded. It was like saying his name had thickened the air around them, making it hard to take a breath.

"Molly says he's still alive," Anna said.

"Right." Yoshi made it clear he didn't think so.

"Anyway, I'd love to get another look at that forest," Anna said. "Why was Hank so mad at me for leaving yesterday? I wasn't gone that long. You found me really fast."

"Gone a long time," Kira said.

Yoshi turned. He spoke to Kira in Japanese, and she answered. Yoshi shook his head, and then questioned Kira closely. Akiko answered him, pointing at the woods and then up to the sky. Anna stirred impatiently. Clearly she needed to know more Japanese words than *midori* and *omoshiroi*.

"What's going on?"

Yoshi turned back to her. "How long do you think you were gone?"

Anna considered this. She had followed the insect for a very short time. Then she got lost, but she figured that out pretty quickly, and the clock thing with the cones didn't take too long to accomplish. Then the hog creature who tried to ambush her and the jawbug attack. That part had *seemed* long, but it couldn't have been more than twenty minutes.

"Maybe an hour?"

"We were gone for five hours," Yoshi said. "The whole afternoon, in fact. Kira and Akiko say we left after lunch and came back at dusk."

"That's impossible," Anna said. She looked down at her wrist, where a watch might be if she had one. She looked up for a sun that wasn't there. But Yoshi was right. She'd wandered off right after lunch and the fire had been burning brightly against the dark gray when they returned. How hadn't she noticed that?

"Given that we're lost in some sort of weird valley where nothing makes sense, maybe we just banish the word *impossible* from our vocab," Yoshi said.

Anna swallowed and tried to laugh. "Yeah." She tried to wrap her head around losing that much time. Kira was folding her paper into an origami shape, her fingers quick and expert.

Kira held up the origami crane. She pointed to the folds. "Time." She twirled the paper creature around.

"It bends and folds," Yoshi said. "Thanks, Professor Einstein."

"Are you saying we fell into some sort of time fold?" Anna asked, touching the origami crane with a tentative finger.

Kira shrugged. "Only answer."

It made her feel strange, like the world was just this shifting, spongy, elastic, changing, spinning thing that could throw you sideways at any moment.

Which, of course, it *was*.

Molly

Since the plane crash, things had moved so fast. There was water to find and food to gather and strange devices to decipher and places they had to get to. Sleep was snatched under an unfamiliar sky. Molly had gotten used to being scared.

This was different.

Cal had stopped her before she'd left the hut.

"Wait."

She turned and met his gaze.

"Memories. Coming fast now. Good, bad. Everyday ordinary, perfect spectacular, horrible terrible."

"How did you know?" Molly whispered.

"You'll get over it."

"Get over what?" Molly asked.

"Being human." Cal turned away, swinging the broken watch.

Now Molly couldn't stop thinking about what he'd said.

How could he know about the memories that kept flooding her here? About the beach in July and a snowstorm on a school day and ice cream after dinner. About a ringing phone in the middle of the night, about a hospital hallway where she watched her mother slide down a wall to crouch with her head in her hands.

When he said "you'll get over it," did he mean she needed to say good-bye to what she felt in those moments? Joy, unimaginable pain. Was she turning . . . *inhuman*?

Or was she just slowly losing her mind?

Whatever was happening to her, Cal *knew*. Was she turning into . . . him?

She couldn't leave the compound until she knew. She had to find a way into his mind, like he'd found a way into hers.

But first she had to tell Hank that there might be help at the end of the valley. That Oliver had said so. She owed Cal that, she owed all of them.

Molly sat with her back against a tree. Javi was helping the Cubs pound seeds into paste. Hank was changing water into gel blocks for storage. She watched as Yoshi turned from Akiko, Kira, and Anna and walked toward her, frowning and intent.

Decisions. When to leave. He was coming to discuss it.

She knew they had to decide whether to tell the Cubs about the time warp. Was it better to leave them with their seed buns and their music and their belief that Lyndon Baines Johnson was still president? A world whose soundtrack was transistor radios playing the Beatles? Where nobody had invented frozen yogurt (she didn't think) or knew who Obi-Wan Kenobi was?

Yoshi crouched down next to her. "We have to go. Today. This morning."

"I was thinking tomorrow."

"How long were we gone yesterday?"

"Long enough for me to approach freak-out territory. Maybe four or five hours?"

"Molly, listen. It felt like less than an hour to me. Anna, too. I think we got caught in some sort of time"—Yoshi hesitated, looking back at where Kira sat sketching—"fold. In the woods out there. Maybe there's more than one. There are magnetic fields, why couldn't there be time fields? We've seen rings of low gravity, perfect circles with stunted trees. So . . . places that stop time? That would explain the whole 1965 thing. We've got to get out of here. I don't want to get rescued and find out it's 2070. Do you?"

Molly pressed her hands on the ground, needing to feel something solid. "No. But you experienced that time loss in the woods. I think we're okay here. We can certainly wait another day."

"Are you kidding me?" Yoshi shot to his feet. "One more day could be another *century*! We don't know how time works here!"

"It's just a feeling . . . I can't explain it."

"You can't *explain* it?" Yoshi looked at her, incredulous. "Whatever happened to Molly-logic? 'Theories'? 'Conjectures'?" He mimicked Molly's serious voice. "Now you're just sitting there . . . *feeling*?"

Yes, because I don't know how much longer I'll feel anything at all.

Yes, because I'm more afraid right now than I've ever been. Because I thought there was a limit to how scared you can get. There isn't.

Molly looked over Yoshi's shoulder at Cal's lean-to. She saw him standing in the threshold, looking at her. Spinning that broken watch.

If she could find out from Cal what would happen, she could know when she was slipping away. She could tell the Killbots that they wouldn't have her for much longer. She could be like her dad, who was so brave at the end. He knew he would die even when her mother refused to face it. He had taken her hand and said there would be a corner of sadness in her heart her whole life, but she would get to live it, and that was everything to him.

She wanted to be that brave.

She wasn't.

Not yet.

Because she had to *know*.

She pressed her hands to her temples. "You always think you're right, Yoshi. You push too hard! I need some time to think, okay?"

"Fine." His voice was icy. "Take your time. But remember, you might be taking way more than you know."

Yoshi

The Cub-Tones were tuning up. Apparently they rehearsed every morning, after they marked the path to the stream. It was one of Hank's rules.

The guy was a dictator. He even had them line up in formation. They were playing a song called "Mr. Tambourine Man" and doing this thing called "chair-stepping," lifting their knees high while they marched. It looked ridiculous, but after a few initial laughs from the Killbots, nobody was even smiling. They were staring, rapt, and tapping their feet, applauding after every song. Maybe it was because they were remembering home. Parades, football games, the Super Bowl.

Yoshi had never been interested in any of those things.

After the marching songs, Hank began something classical, and Dana and Akiko joined in with their flutes. Yoshi knew this piece. He'd been forced to go to concerts with his father.

He had spent the time twitching with impatience and longing for his phone, which he'd been ordered to leave at home.

The music soared here. It filled his chest with longing. He didn't think that out of all the things he missed from his old life, he'd ever miss Bach.

Even Cal had left his hut and was pacing in a circle around it. The boy marked time with one hand in the air. Javi had warned the others that Cal would be unusual but . . . wow. Yoshi felt a twinge of pity for him, for the green veins that pulsed in his neck and the wild gleam in his eyes.

Yoshi was done. He wouldn't stick around long enough to become *that*. He had taken some seed cakes and water cubes and secreted them in his pack. He had pocketed the Killbots' antigravity device. He was ready to go.

He couldn't just walk out, though. He needed to tell someone he was going so that they wouldn't look for him. Someone who would understand his decision.

Kira appeared at his elbow. "Akiko is happy. She gets to play with someone really good."

Yoshi shrugged.

"You think Anna is pretty," she said.

He swiveled. "What?"

"You said it, when you were bitten by the scorpion back in the desert. It was a kind of truth serum. Also Molly, and Akiko, and even me. All of us, pretty." Kira smiled. "I just wanted to say thank you for the compliment."

Yoshi felt the blush begin in his cheeks and spread to his

fingertips, which tingled with his humiliation. Well, here was another reason to take off.

"Would have been better if you'd said it without the scorpion," she added.

Yoshi didn't answer. He still felt the blood beating in his cheeks.

"You also said that your parents don't want you."

He took a breath. "They don't."

"So maybe you think we don't want you. But we do. Take a look around, Yoshi-chan. Whatever you're thinking, you're wrong."

"I'm not thinking anything."

"A frog in a well does not know the great sea."

"Don't go all Magical Asian on me," Yoshi said. "I'm a *hafu*, remember?"

"If half of you gets it, that's a start," Kira replied with a grin.

Yoshi knew the Japanese proverb. It was a kind of warning against thinking you know everything when you only see what's around you. "Are you saying that I'm the frog?"

"We are all frogs. We have to find a way to see outside of the machine," Kira said. "It's like Molly says all the time, the English word. *Conjectures*. Why did you get lost in the forest? Why does the stream change its course? Why does the ridge disappear? The answer could be that the woods themselves don't want us to leave."

"Woods can't make decisions," Yoshi said.

"Of course they can," Kira said. "Plants make decisions all

the time. They turn toward a light source. Trees decay and seeds travel on air. Why couldn't plants twist and turn in order to fool us?"

"Because plants can't think," Yoshi said.

"No, but there is some kind of intelligence here that can. Remember we are trapped in a well. Someone built it. If they can make all of this, they can change it," Kira said. "The growth cycles are off, right? Normally when we move through the forest we notice things, the shape of the trees or rocks to help us remember where we are. If there are time folds out there, they are constantly manipulating time. You can be aware, you can think you know where you're going, but you might never reach it." She gazed out into the forest. "I think it's possible to get lost forever. Either in the forest, or in time. I wouldn't want to be lost by myself."

It was like Kira knew he was thinking of leaving.

"You'd just have to make sure you didn't get lost," Yoshi said. "Once a person climbed the ridge, they'd know where they were."

"Above the trees?" Kira looked up dubiously. "These trees, you can't get above." It was true, the tree canopy was so dense it would be close to impossible to climb through.

Yoshi had a sudden thought. "Those trees we saw—the ones with big trunks that narrow and widen, and the upside-down ones . . . maybe it was because they would slow their growth, then speed up again. Maybe they're *inside* time folds. So if you're in the woods, you just avoid them."

Kira shook her head. "You can't know if that's the only danger. This place is manufactured to trap and confuse. Totally artificial. Which reminds me. There are no rocks."

"No rocks?" Yoshi thought back to his walk through the forest. He hadn't seen a single boulder or stone. Anna had used pinecones to make her directional clock, not rocks. "That's strange."

"Not really," Kira said. "Rocks come from molten magma deep in the earth. But we're not dealing with regular processes here. We knew that already. This forest was *built*. Created by someone or something and maintained by robots, just like everything else we've seen. We know we're on Earth, but it's like . . . a biome laid on top of another biome. Or something."

"You sound like Anna."

"Anna's not the only one who knows about science."

Yoshi stood still for a moment, thinking. "Then why when I missed the snakehog did my katana clang against a rock?"

Kira cocked her head. "Are you sure it was a rock?"

Yoshi thought back to the encounter. It was hard, because he'd been lost in the heat of the moment, in his terror and determination. The missed blow had traveled up his arm, making it shake. The katana had hit something just buried by the dirt that had been stirred up by the animal's charge.

Metal. Something made of metal, underneath the forest floor.

Molly

Molly spied Hank across the compound, stacking blue cubes for the fire. She crossed the compound and began to help him without saying a word.

"Thanks."

"No problem."

"It's funny, how you all talk," he said. "'No problem.' 'Thanks, dude.' 'LOL.' 'Be chill.' Is that a New York thing?"

"I guess so. Hank . . . what do you think happened to Cal?"

Hank paused for the briefest of seconds. "I think the pressure of this place got to him. It broke his mind."

"But what about the attack from the creature?"

"It was awful. Ferocious. Terrifying. The wound healed, but his mind didn't."

"Are you *sure* it healed? What about the green . . . rashy thing?"

"It doesn't cause him pain. It's like a scar."

Molly picked up a gel cube. "If he can't help it, why are you so angry at him?"

Hank sighed. "I'm not angry now. I was. He tried to break his clarinet. He would have smashed my oboe, too, if I hadn't gotten away. He went for Dana's flute. I was playing Mozart, his favorite piece, the adagio movement, Clarinet Concerto in A Major. I mean, we worked together on it, we played it. We were the music guys, total squares, in band *and* orchestra. Best friends. And then he tried to smash it. Destroy it."

"But you say he was out of his mind, so—"

"No." Hank turned and looked at her. His gray eyes blazed with sorrow and anger. "It was *before* he lost his mind. He was still my friend then. And he knew what music meant to me. To all of us. But he couldn't play anymore, so he tried to take it all away from all of us."

"When you were playing before, it bothered him. Why is that?"

"Music agitates him sometimes. We don't know why."

"Does he ever make sense? I mean, how does he communicate?"

"Communicate what? That he's crazy?" Hank tossed a cube. "Look, I know you're trying to help. But you have to believe me. I tried to reach him. Over and over and over again. The only time he's calm is when he's with Dana."

Molly hesitated. "I need to tell you something," she said.

"Okay," he said cautiously.

"I really think you all need to come with us," she said.

Hank was already shaking his head. "Abandon the compound? We worked hard on it. It's survival."

"We were told that there could be help out there for someone like Cal."

"Someone *like* Cal? What do you mean?"

"Our friend Oliver. He . . . it's hard to explain, but we think whoever built this place spoke to us through him. He said that the building could help me."

"But you aren't like Cal."

"Not yet," Molly said. She took a deep breath. "I was bitten by a dreadful duck, too."

Hank sat back on his heels. "Whoa. I'm sorry."

"It's not that bad yet," Molly said, which wasn't quite the truth. "Would you . . . look at it and tell me if it's like what Cal had?"

Hank nodded. She pulled the neck of her T-shirt to show him the green scar. She saw him swallow.

"It's just like his, isn't it?"

Hank nodded. "It started to grow, travel down his neck and his back . . . "

"Oh." Molly pressed her fingers against the wound.

"I'm really sorry," Hank said. "Just because Cal's scar spread, it doesn't mean yours will."

Molly let the fabric fall. "It's okay. I know help is out there."

"Help is up there." Hank pointed to the sky. "If we stay together, we'll see a plane eventually. We can't be *that* far off the map. Now that two planes have gone down, they'll work even harder to find us."

"It's not distance I'm worried about," Molly said. "It's time."

"What do you mean?"

Molly wasn't good at breaking bad news. She remembered the moment her mother told her that her father had died. She remembered how it seemed to take forever for her mother to get out the words, how agonizing it was, waiting for that blow to fall, knowing she was living in a moment in which there was still hope.

"I think you might be in a time warp," she blurted.

"What?" Hank laughed a little as he placed a cube carefully on the pile.

"You've been here longer than you think," she said. "While you've been here in the woods, time was moving. Faster than you know."

"How much faster?"

"Over fifty years have passed since your plane went down."

At first Hank's face had no expression, as though she'd suddenly hit him on the head with a shovel. Then he rocked back on his heels. "Fifty *years*?"

"We're from the future. I mean, *your* future. Our present." Molly wished she could see his eyes, but he turned his face away as she was talking.

Hank stared down at his hands. He took a deep, shuddering breath. "Fifty years," he repeated. "That's nuts. We haven't aged fifty years!"

"I know. The thing about time? We don't really get it. How it works. There's this area of study called quantum physics—"

"Wait. So this means you're from the future."

"No, we're from the present. You're already *in* the future. I don't know how the time warp works. I don't know how far it extends, or even if it's a physical *thing*, like a force field."

"Do you have time machines, then? I mean . . . " Hank waved a hand. "Out there. In the future? My future, your present?"

"No! We can't move through time. But some scientists say that all time could be taking place simultaneously, only we can't break through. I mean, in the multiverse there could be many dimensions, more than we know on Earth, right?"

"The multiverse?"

"Sure. There's more than one universe, they think. And so there could be multiple time-space continuums—"

"Were you in the science club or something?"

"Robotics."

"Robots? Like in *The Jetsons*?"

"I don't know what that is, but you create software to make—"

"Software?"

Molly sighed. "Computers are really small now, and practically everyone has one of their own." She paused as Hank shook his head in disbelief. "We learn how to write code in school, and— Oh, never mind. My point is, even physicists don't know this stuff for sure. They can design a theory to explain how the universe works, but they can't say for sure what the big picture is. They can get the mechanics right, but what if they think it's like a car, but it's really an elephant?"

"But an elephant is a living thing, not a machine."

Molly raked her hand through her hair. "Okay, bad example. I'm trying to tell you that a time warp is possible."

She could tell he was hardly listening.

"Did the Russians ever drop the A-bomb? Did we? Is that why we're in this place?" Hank asked.

"No. Everybody kind of agreed that using nuclear weapons was stupid. I mean, not everybody in the whole world, but we kind of kept a lid on it for a really long time."

"So. Peace on Earth?"

"Not exactly." Molly thought a moment. There was so much she could tell him. There was so much she didn't want to tell him.

"If you're fifty years in the future, there must be all kinds of new technology to find missing planes," Hank said.

"Sure. Satellite technology and stuff. But I think this place is hidden, somehow. Obviously there's technology here that's way beyond what we know."

"Sooner or later, they'll find us, though," Hank said.

"They haven't found you after fifty years!"

"But the longer we're here, the better the technology gets," Hank pointed out. "Our job is to stay alive until they do. If you stayed here with us, with your engineering skills and your devices, we could really make this place like a fortress."

"Our best way to survive is to keep moving," Molly said firmly. "Yours, too."

Hank shook his head. "My job is to protect my crew. We tried so many times. The big beaks attack. The snakehogs. But worse than that . . . something happens to us. We get confused. We get lost. I can't lose another Cub. You'll see. If you do leave, you'll be back here after a day or two. You'll never make it out of the forest."

"I don't believe that," Molly said. "And don't you think your crew deserves a chance to decide for themselves?"

Hank looked over to the makeshift table where Pammy, Kimberly, and Dana were working with Stu and Drew and Crash, pounding berries into paste, drying flowers and fruit, and chatting.

"I can't tell them," he said. "Why should they know this until they have to? Like I said, my job is to protect them."

He stood, dusting off his hands. "Going is your choice. But Kim was right—you guys could use some rest. Just stay one more day. That will give us a chance to gather supplies for you, operate the water-changer and make more cubes. Then we'll pack you up with as much as you can carry and guide you as far as the stream."

"One more day," Molly agreed.

19

Javi

Javi liked it here. He was afraid to admit it to Molly. He liked the smell of the trees and he liked being in a place where there were chores to do and everyone pitched in. Which was funny, because at home he was always trying to get *out* of doing chores, and his mother would have to give him that look that meant *Do it now, mister* to get him to take out the garbage or make his bed.

Here the chores were pleasant, somehow. Sweeping the dirt with a rake made out of a branch with stiff bristled cones tied on with twine. Grinding seeds into paste. Dana was even teaching him how to sew with a needle made of bone, and thread made from some kind of fibrous root.

It amazed him that they'd figured out so much. He was a city kid, and he never knew what plants could do. Dana's mother had grown herbs and flowers and was always giving her special teas and tinctures instead of medicine.

"Sounds like your mom's a hippie," Javi had said, and Dana had said mildly that her mom was actually quite slender. Javi guessed they didn't have hippies in 1965. He had put his foot in it. Again.

Javi hadn't realized how tired he was. Tired of escaping from shredder birds and tanglevines. Tired of being hungry. Tired of snatching sleep while you worried about yet another attack from a creature you hadn't met before. Tired of fear and worry and terror that left you shaking for whole minutes afterward and trying to hide it.

He liked feeling safe.

He hadn't realized that he'd missed music until he had it again. Practice for these kids wasn't a chore at all, it was more like the *reward* for getting the chores done, something they looked forward to every day. Hank's oboe dipped and soared, and Dana's flute and Kimberly's piccolo were like silver lines traced in the air. Even Crash played the glockenspiel with such delicacy it sounded like tinkling bells. Kimberly wrote music, too, so there was always new stuff to practice.

He could get used to this. Maybe their plan to get to the end of the valley was dangerous and bound to fail. Maybe if they stayed put, whoever was building this place would just get tired and leave them alone. Or lift the mist and allow a plane to drift into the airspace and not destroy it. Allow it to see them.

Javi had been the one to push to get to the end of the valley. He'd thought it would save Molly, save all of them.

Maybe he'd been wrong. Maybe they had more options than they knew.

Maybe nobody else had to die.

Molly sat down next to him as he tried to master the stitch Dana had taught him. The curtains on the lean-tos needed to be replaced. He had trouble getting the material to cooperate. It kept bunching and twisting. Dana had made it look so easy. It had taken him forever just to do one row.

"Yoshi thinks we should leave right away," Molly murmured. "He thinks he and Anna were caught in a time warp yesterday out in the woods."

"Yesterday?" Javi suddenly felt confused for a second. Hadn't Anna gone missing a couple of days earlier?

"Whenever," Molly said. She looked confused for a minute, too, but then the expression passed. There were small beads of sweat on her collarbone, and she yanked at her shirt collar. "Anyway, Hank tried to talk me into staying. I said yes, but . . . I don't know, I keep thinking about what Yoshi said."

"It does feel safe here," Javi said, jabbing at the material. Oh, if he just held the cloth taut, then went in at an angle, it worked perfectly, just as Dana had said. He let out a sigh of satisfaction.

"Hey, I hate to interrupt your *sewing*, but we have decisions to make."

Javi looked up and met Molly's impatient gaze. "You can

mock it, but I'm learning a useful skill. Look around. These guys really made something here."

"Sure," Molly said. "I give them that. But they're not any closer to getting out."

Javi bent over his work again. "I'm just saying Hank has a point. We don't know for sure what's at the end of the valley. We only know what zombie-Oliver told us. It's not like there was a box on the map that said, *Rescue is here.* What if that weird nightmare alien lives there?"

"There are a thousand what-ifs," Molly argued. "If we looked at all of them, we'd never move."

"But that's my point," Javi said. "The one option we didn't consider was not moving at all. Remember when we were little and our moms told us that if we ever got separated, just stay put? That it was the best way to find us again?"

"You can't compare *all this* to getting lost in Target!"

"I'm not! I'm just saying! Every time we go to a new biome, we lose someone!"

Molly stood, her fists clenched. There was something wild in her eyes that he didn't understand. "What about Oliver? He told us he'd meet us there!"

"That wasn't Oliver!" Javi felt his throat burn with unshed tears. He knew, right then, that he'd lost hope. "Oliver is dead. He was sucked under the sand, and you made the decision not to go after him *until it was too late.*"

It was the worst thing he could have said to her. It was like something terrible inside him, all his fear and anger and grief, had packed inside the words and sent them shooting out of his mouth.

Funny thing about words. Once they're in the air, they're gone.

They stared at each other, shocked. They'd never spoken to each other this way. Javi could feel the strong base of their friendship splinter into cracks as Molly stalked off.

20

Molly

She felt Javi's words like a bruise. Like he had punched her.

Her fault Oliver was dead.

But he's not! her heart cried.

He was alive; she knew he was. He had to be!

"Hey!" Kimberly broke into her thoughts. "The idea is to pull the weeds, not the crops."

Molly looked down at the green shoot in her hand. She'd left Javi and spotted Kimberly working in the tuber patch. She offered to help, even though the last time she'd interacted with a plant was during her second-grade cabbage project. "Oh. Sorry!"

"It's okay." Kimberly held up a fistful of green. "Weeds." She pointed to the ground. "Tubers."

"Got it." Molly crouched down and pulled a weed from the tuber plot. Kimberly had been surprised to hear that Molly didn't have a garden at home. The fact that they could pull tubers from under the ground instead of out of a produce bin was still remarkable to Molly.

Oliver was a city kid, too. He lived only a few blocks from Molly. She knew his mom and dad. Molly willed herself not to think of Oliver's red-haired little brother and his cat, Zazie.

Then the world dropped away and she felt memory take her over.

Summer. She sat on Oliver's front stoop, the stone warm against her legs. Oliver grinned at her. There was juice from a grape ice pop on his chin. She could feel the sun on her back. Her hands were sticky, and her mouth felt full of cherry flavor from the ice pop she was devouring. A woman walking by smiled at her and said, "That looks good."

Molly could hear it, she could feel it, she could taste it. A summer day in Brooklyn.

She shook her head to make the memory go away. She didn't want to remember Oliver like that, happy and alive. She didn't want to think about the decision she'd made at that horrible moment.

Yoshi had tried to save Oliver, had allowed himself to get sucked underneath the sand, had groped for him, had searched until his air ran out and his heart had almost burst. He'd come up again, taken a breath, gone down again, and when he came up again without Oliver, gasping, worn out . . .

In a flash, Molly had decided that Yoshi *could not* try again. They would lose him, too. There was a monster under the sand, a beast that could have taken Yoshi or any one of them at any moment. They were weak from the lack of water and food.

She had said no. No more rescue attempts.

They had moved on, they had found water, and then Molly made the decision to go back. Instead, Oliver had found them. The robotic Oliver with the dead eyes and voice.

Molly tried to push it all out of her brain. Concentrate on weeds.

Everything was peaceful in the compound. Musical instruments were lined up on the table, and Stu and Drew were busy polishing and blowing into them, not making music, just checking stops and keys.

Hank sat with his back to the big flat log that served as a seating area for the group, teaching Akiko a song. He played the tune and waited for her to repeat it on her flute. It was a complicated melody and she kept getting it wrong, but they would both laugh and she would try to follow him again.

Javi and Dana had finished hanging all the new vine curtains for the lean-tos. Everyone had eaten lunch. For some reason Molly couldn't remember what she'd had, but her belly felt full and she was almost drowsy.

"I think we got them all," Kimberly said, standing up and dusting off her hands. "Thanks for the help."

"When will these tubers be ready to eat?" Molly asked.

"Maybe another two weeks," Kimberly answered. "Don't worry, we have plenty in storage."

As they walked up to the others, Hank was showing Akiko the different handmade reeds he'd fashioned. He played his oboe and the sound came out high and sharp. Molly didn't know music, but even she knew he wasn't making those sounds on purpose.

"Hey, daddy-o, can you cool it? That noise is gonna break my glasses!" Crash called. "And I'm not wearing any!"

Molly didn't think it was *so* bad. There was something different and interesting about the sound.

Akiko examined Cal's half-broken clarinet. She put it to her mouth and tried to mimic the sound that Hank was making. Kira laughed and clapped her hands over her ears. Hank grinned and kept going. The music skittered and jumped. It didn't so much swell in sound as punctuate the air like raindrops. Or shredder bird beaks. *Peck, peck, peck. Swoop, swoop, swoop.* Kimberly put her fingers in her ears.

Molly's head filled with the notes. It was like staring at a math test she hadn't studied for, and yet the numbers *almost* made sense. It was the song she couldn't get out of her head, but couldn't remember the words to.

It was familiar and it was strange, all at once.

"I'm losing it," Molly muttered.

Cal emerged from the hut and stared at Hank and Akiko.

"Significant shift!" he suddenly shouted.

The notes arranged themselves into something new. Molly didn't hear strange, scratchy music anymore. She was on the edge of grasping something. Not music, but . . . *concepts*. Not notes, but *meaning*.

Significant shift. The thought buzzed around in her mind. Which was strange, because she had no idea what it meant.

She stood stock-still while Cal looked across the compound at her. Their eyes met, and his were strange and alien, and she was so afraid her whole body began to shake.

Hank played another burst, and the gel cubes around the fire flared with light, then dimmed.

Molly swallowed, but her voice was still a croak. "Hank? Can you play those notes again?"

"Not really notes," Hank said. "More like a series of glissandos."

"Whatever!"

Hank blew into the oboe. The sound wasn't the same, but it was close to what it had been. Akiko picked up the pitch and blew into the broken clarinet, trying to match it.

The cubes flared again, a bit lower this time. On the log beside Hank, the Cub-Tones' alien device also came to life. The glowing symbols along the ring pulsed in strange rhythms.

"Did you see that?" Molly asked. "The music . . . "

"It's not music," Kimberly said with a laugh. "It's noise."

Dana looked over at Molly, her gaze sharp. "Cal says that. Music noise music noise. All the time."

"He's trying to tell you something," Molly said. "All of us. The music affects the devices somehow. Maybe other things. Maybe we don't know everything the devices do." She reached into her pocket for the Killbots' device. It wasn't there.

"*Omoshiroi,*" Akiko said.

"Interesting," Kira translated for the Cubs.

"I can't find the device I was holding," Molly said. "Does anyone have it?"

"Countdown," Cal said. "Four five six is not the frequency."

Hank spun around. "What is the frequency, Cal?"

Cal didn't look at Hank. He looked up at the sky. "Four five six is not the frequency."

Hank spun back in frustration. "Why are you so *useless*?"

"Stop it!" Kimberly stepped forward. Her face was flushed. "Stop *punishing* him! He can't help it! You were his best friend!"

For a long moment, nobody spoke. Molly had never seen Kimberly snap at anyone like that. Especially Hank. She snuck a look at Javi. Her own feelings were still smarting from their argument earlier that . . . morning? Afternoon?

Funny, she couldn't remember how long it had been. Molly glanced up at the treetops, hoping to glean some sense of the time. All she could see was an endless ceiling of mist.

Akiko murmured something. Javi turned to her. "What did you say?"

"Yoshi," Akiko said. "Where did he go?"

"Not again," Hank said with a groan. "Doesn't that guy ever stay put?"

"He's probably hunting," Javi said.

Kira shook her head sadly. "Or gone," she said. "Maybe for good."

Anna

The way to defeat the sense of being lost is to not feel lost.

Anna wasn't lost. She was just . . . discovering new ways to get where she was going.

Kimberly hadn't been exaggerating when she said the rust-colored moss was hard to spot. Anna kept getting turned around, and she was already going in circles. When she saw the moss, she went in the opposite direction. She knew Yoshi would keep heading away from the compound.

She had to find him. Kira had warned the others with her few English words and a lot of pantomime that Yoshi had likely headed off on his own. And he'd taken the Killbots' device. Kira was afraid he would simply keep going. Get to the end of the valley by himself.

That couldn't happen. He'd never make it.

Hopefully Molly, Hank, and the others wouldn't notice she was gone for a while. It shouldn't take long. She knew where Yoshi was headed. She had to talk to him, had to convince him not to leave.

At last she arrived at the bramble bushes she'd plunged into to get away from the snakehog. That meant the stream was close, and the ridge was beyond the stream. Anna wrapped the ends of her shirt around her hands and tried to push her way through. They seemed to have grown thicker and taller since the last time, or maybe panic had made her not notice how sharp the barbs were. Eventually, she dropped to her knees, where the twisting trunks were free of thorns. She had to practically crawl on her belly.

She heard a strange noise, a clicking, scratching noise. It seemed to rise from beneath the earth. A burrowing creature? She moved faster, grabbing the ground to propel herself along. Chunks of dirt flew into her face as she scrabbled forward. Finally, she rolled out onto the clearing. She looked behind her quickly, but no creature had followed her.

Yoshi was standing yards away. He looked at her and raised one eyebrow, a skill Anna had always wanted to have.

"Nice entrance. You're looking good."

"Thanks." Anna sprang to her feet and dusted off her knees. She walked over to join Yoshi, who was standing by the skeleton of the snakehog.

"Wow, his bones are picked clean already," Anna said.

Yoshi seemed skeptical. "Well, it's been a couple of days," he said. "Plenty of predators out here."

Days? Anna tried to remember. Meanwhile, Yoshi went back to what he was doing, poking his katana into the tree grove, then quickly sliding it back out.

"What are you doing?"

"Stirring a wasp's nest."

"And this is a good idea because . . . ?"

"Don't worry, the jawbugs aren't leaving the grove. They perceive the threat, then adjust when it leaves. I think there's a giant nest in the cave."

"There's a cave?"

"You can see it when they come out of it. I'm just trying to figure it out. I think this might be where 'the Thing' that the Cub-Tones are so afraid of is."

"Oh, it makes total sense that you're trying to provoke an apex predator so it will get angry and eat us," Anna said.

"I'm not an idiot," Yoshi said. "Obviously, I'm not going in there until I know what I'm dealing with."

"You shouldn't go in there at all," Anna said.

"Listen to this." Yoshi rapped the hilt of his sword against the ground. "Do you hear that? It's metal. There's something under the dirt. I think it's a tunnel." Yoshi squatted close to the ground and put his hand down. "You can feel vibrations, like something big is moving down there."

Anna knelt to feel the ground. "I thought I heard

something belowground when I was crawling before. Maybe we should come back with the others."

"That could be a plan if the Cubs weren't all basically useless."

"That's not fair," Anna said. "Is that why you want to leave?"

"Who said I was leaving? Kira?" Yoshi's face darkened with anger. "She talks too much."

"She was worried. Why did you take the device?" she asked.

"Because I wanted to test a theory."

Anna shot to her feet. "But you're leaving! You're going on without us! How could you do that to us?"

"What?" Yoshi looked up at her. "Is that what you think I'm like? That I'd steal something that helps us survive?"

"How am I supposed to know what you'd do?" Anna demanded. "You're so angry all the time! Don't you ever just *talk* to people?"

"We're talking right now!"

"No, we're not. We're arguing!"

Anna wanted to howl in frustration. How could she tell this angry boy that they needed him? In a way that wouldn't embarrass him? That was the trick.

The breeze lifted Anna's hair. The evening wind was coming.

No. It was too early for the *yokaze*. It was early afternoon. Wasn't it?

The wind was rhythmic. It beat against her ears.

"ANNA!" Yoshi bellowed, and started to rise, already reaching for his sword.

She felt a shadow on her and had only a split second to look up and see the raptor bearing down on her. She saw a bright green eye shot with yellow, and sharp claws extended from a powerful body the size of a large dog.

Anna screamed. She saw Yoshi's desperate face as he strained to reach her, but it was too late. The raptor plucked her off the forest floor.

Anna watched in disbelief as the ground receded. Yoshi was just a dot, his katana in a backswing, aiming for a target that was already several hundred feet in the air and rising higher.

It had happened so fast! Adrenaline flooded her body as the bird's talons dug into her shoulders. She was afraid to twist or beat her fists against it. What if it dropped her?

The huge beating wings were like drumbeats. They weaved through the topmost branches at high speed. Anna hugged her legs against her chest, afraid they'd slam against a branch. Then they burst through the top of the canopy into gray formless sky. Anna blinked, trying to get her bearings. From here she could see through occasional breaks in the canopy. She saw the compound in the middle of the forest. She glimpsed the thin ribbon of the stream. Away in the distance, the ridge. And as the raptor rose she saw beyond the ridge . . . more forest. Acres and acres of forest. And maybe, at the very end . . . something gray? Something that moved? What moved and shimmered like that?

Water. So much water it looked like an ocean.

It was like having access to an aerial map. Through her panic she tried to make sense of it. If she lived through this, it could be helpful. Parts of the forest were slightly blurred. Something close to what Javi had described when he'd activated that cloaking device back in the desert. Distortions. There were areas where the trees wavered or shimmered. Lines of barely visible force bisecting the forest. *Like a bicycle wheel*, she thought, *with a glint at the center.*

Time folds. She could actually *see* them.

She could hardly wait to tell the others—except that the giant raptor was no doubt bringing her to its nest, where it would kill her and then eat her. She just hoped it would be fast.

Anna's teeth chattered. Maybe it would be better to just drop. All the way to the earth. That would be quick, right? *Smash.*

The bird shifted a bit, descended, and made a lazy circle above a field littered with broken pieces of machinery. She strained for a better view, but the bird descended faster, swooping back into the trees, its beating wings ruffling the leaves.

She could see its nest ahead, a mass of twisted sticks sitting in a forked tree. Baby raptors the size of Thanksgiving turkeys sat in it. Mouths open.

Waiting for dinner.

Something sliced the air, arcing toward them. An arrow. It overshot them and fell just short of the nest, disappearing into the leaves.

Anna peered down. Yoshi was right below her, fitting another arrow into the bow.

"Yoshi!" she screamed. Was he crazy? If he shot the raptor, she'd plummet to the ground!

Another arrow arced into the air, this one well below them. Anna learned something new. Yoshi was a really bad shot.

But the arrow came within a few feet of the nest. It hit the trunk and skittered in a downward fall. The raptor let out a furious cry.

Yoshi was shooting at the *nest*.

Another arrow came flying. The raptor wheeled, its claws digging harder into Anna's shoulders. It made a beeline for the nest. Below, Yoshi held up something in the air.

The gravity device.

Now she understood. The raptor would fly lower to protect her babies. She would attack Yoshi. That would put Anna in range of the device.

Anna's mind worked at lightning speed. The raptor had to be low enough so that if it dropped her, Yoshi would activate the device and she wouldn't fall. Yoshi would rise. They would meet in the middle.

Hopefully not in the raptor's beak.

22

Yoshi

Was he imagining the evil he saw in the green-yellow eye of the raptor?

He'd gotten its attention, anyway. Yoshi fitted another arrow into the bow. He knew the raptor was capable of amazing speed, so his timing had to be flawless.

Hang on, Anna.

Well, maybe do the opposite. Let go. But not until he was ready for her.

Yoshi let the last arrow fly, aiming straight for the nest. With a terrible cry, the raptor shot downward, placing its body between Yoshi and the nest and heading for him. At the same time, the bird released Anna. It had more important things to do with its talons.

Anna plummeted toward the ground, screaming. Yoshi

dropped the bow and twisted the gravity device, pressing the glowing symbols.

He felt the lurch as gravity lowered. Yoshi bent his legs and pushed off, shooting into the air.

Her free fall slowed by the antigravity, Anna was able to grab on to a nearby branch. Yoshi bounced off a bulbous tree trunk, higher, closer to Anna. She was hugging the tree, her face red, tears streaking the grime.

Confused, the raptor circled overhead.

"Just stay still," Yoshi said, wrapping a bungee cord around Anna's waist.

He figured the raptor could see them. As a bird of prey, its eyesight would have to be supreme. But he was hoping that its instinct to protect the nest overrode everything else. Failing that, if it came after them, maybe the low gravity would slow it down enough that he would be a match for it. He kept the device on and his sword at the ready.

Two heart-pounding minutes later, the raptor finally stopped circling over the nest and took off.

Anna took a deep, shuddering breath. "I owe you two now."

"We should be safe to float down," Yoshi said. "You ready?"

"I've never been more ready to hit the ground," Anna said. "Softly."

Yoshi released his grip on the branch and they slowly

floated down. Once they'd set down, he turned off the device and unhooked the bungee cord.

Anna looked around nervously. "Have you seen the triple D?"

"More than one, actually, while I was jumping," Yoshi said. "Looked like a whole family. They were going the opposite way. Here's the thing. They weren't interested in me."

"You don't taste good, huh?" Anna said, dusting off her pants. She pressed a hand to her shoulder. Her fingers came away bloody.

Yoshi turned her around to examine it. "Your shirt is in bad shape, but the cuts are superficial. You'll be okay. But we should get some of Dana's magic cream on it."

They heard the sound of something moving, and Yoshi pulled her closer to the tree. They watched as a triple D moved through the forest, followed by another. And another. Anna stuffed her fist in her mouth. They were terrifying creatures, tall and feathered, with long beaks like twin razors.

"It's okay," Yoshi whispered. "They know we're here. They're ignoring us. Maybe they're not hungry. Or we're not a threat."

Anna let out a breath. "I know what this is. They're migrating."

"Lucky for us," Yoshi said. "But why?"

"I don't know. I saw pretty far when I was up there," Anna said. "And the forest seems to stretch for miles." She described the distortions she'd seen in the forest around the compound. "The air was wavering," she said. "Almost like . . . cracks."

"*Omoshiroi*. And we're going to have to walk right through that area to get back."

Anna looked sideways at Yoshi. "So, you *are* going back to the compound?"

"Of course," he said. He felt his mouth tighten in just the way his father's did when he was angry. Why didn't Anna know he would return? Sure, he had wondered if he could get to the building and save the day with just himself and his sword, but he would never *abandon* them. "We have to dress your wound, don't we?"

Anna pointed to some rusty moss on a trunk, and they turned that way. "But you *wanted* to leave," Anna said.

"I thought about it." Yoshi pushed aside a branch and they slithered through. "I thought I could go faster on my own. I'm tired of being told what to do."

"We can't make it without you, Yoshi," Anna said. "You're the bravest out of all of us. Your courage makes us braver."

"That's not true," Yoshi said, but he felt better just hearing it.

They walked in silence for at least a mile. Then Yoshi suddenly stopped. Ahead was a field of short, spiky grass. It was littered with metal bodies.

Worker robots, worn and rusted and missing parts. Some looked as though they'd been blasted apart, their seams melted.

Yoshi and Anna stopped, surveying the creepy scene.

"The robots . . . it's like a junkyard," Yoshi said.

"No. It's a battlefield," Anna said in a hushed voice.

Anna was always the first person to say how robots don't think; they're programmed. They don't have feelings. But this expanse of broken metal made even her look distressed.

Yoshi walked a few feet ahead, kicking through the metal. It had made him feel sad to see the robots like that. It's not like he was fond of them or anything. But there had been a busy diligence about them. They weren't out to harm anything. They got in the way, and they ganged up if you got between them and a task, but they were programmed to work, not kill. So in a way, they were peaceful. Which was more than he could say for the rest of the creatures in this crazy place.

"It's like they were all lured here and massacred," Anna said. "I mean, I can hear Molly in my head saying, *Where's your evidence for that?* But still. It just feels that way."

"I'll tell you what the evidence is," Yoshi said. "The robots are melted. There was some kind of intense heat here. Something big happened."

"Another mystery." Anna shivered. "It feels late. We should get back."

They kept on walking. The stream was near, more of a trickle than the section where they had dived underneath. They crossed it quickly and the ground sloped sharply upward. As they crested the rise they saw that they were behind the grove of upside-down trees.

"Yoshi? Come and see this."

Anna was standing by a tree at the very edge of the grove. The tree had fallen and broken in half. She brushed away dirt from the trunk.

She traced the lines in the wood. "They have concentric rings, just like regular trunks."

"Marking time," Yoshi said.

"Kind of," Anna said. "Dendrochronology is the measurement of time by counting tree rings. Growth changes seasonally, so one ring indicates one year. Except look at how these lines wobble, stop and start. That's because of the time warping. But see here?" She placed a finger on a small notch in the wood. "This is a knife mark," she said. "Someone was trying to count the rings. And here . . . see the little flourish at the end? Like the tail on a quarter note?"

"I guess," Yoshi said.

"Just like the notations in the book I saw, the ones *Hank* made about the tuber crop yields."

"We know Hank has been here before. This was where Cal got bit by the triple D," Yoshi said.

"But why was he keeping track of time here? Or trying to. He never mentioned it." Anna's eyes narrowed in thought. "Look at the marks. He *knew* that large chunks of time had passed."

"But how can you know about a time warp if you're in it?" Yoshi asked.

"You can't." Anna thumped the trunk. "Unless you're the one doing it."

23

Molly

Molly sat on the floor of Cal's hut. She wasn't sure how long she'd been there. The twilight today seemed to last forever, the sky hanging low with mist. She'd been quiet for a long time. She hoped her presence—and her silence—would get Cal used to her.

He, too, sat, his fingers drumming something on his leg. "Sounds, words, sounds, words."

"What?" Molly asked.

"Sounds."

She heard birdsong and leaves rustling. The usual noises of the woods. "I'm a city girl," she said. "I miss the sound of traffic. The hum and the whoosh."

"Hum. Hands on the ground."

She put her hands on the hard-packed dirt. Whatever she

was supposed to hear or feel, she couldn't get it. "What are you trying to tell me?"

Cal didn't answer. He hummed instead, a tuneless noise that reminded her of Hank playing the oboe without a reed.

Suddenly, he leaned in closer to her and cocked his head. "Breakdown is coming."

Molly leaned forward. This was it, this was what she wanted to know. "What did your breakdown feel like?" she whispered. Did it feel like what she was feeling? That something was taking her over? "It happened suddenly, right? Did you have some kind of warning?"

"Intruder takeover!" he suddenly shouted.

Molly slumped backward. If Cal didn't make sense, it didn't make sense for her to go to him for answers. She couldn't help trying, though.

He pushed the watch across the ground toward her. She picked it up and examined the cracked face. "It's broken. I know."

"Can't stop time," he said.

"Is that a joke? Why did you break it?"

"Stuck like glue."

"You can't glue it back together, dude," Molly said. "You broke it."

The door opened, and Yoshi and Anna tumbled in.

Molly scrambled to her feet. "Yoshi, where have you been? We've been freaking out."

"You thought I left for good," Yoshi said.

"I knew you wouldn't abandon us," Molly said. "But a few more minutes and I was on my way out to find you." *A few minutes?* She frowned, trying to think. How long *had* it been since Kira announced that Yoshi had left?

"We've been gone for hours, Molly!" Anna cried. "Maybe even longer than that."

"You left, too?" Molly asked. "But you were with us just a moment . . . Wait, what do you mean *hours*?"

Cal started to drum both hands on the ground. "Manipulation transition!"

"Let's go," Molly murmured. "I don't want to upset him."

As soon as they were outside, she turned to them. "What happened?"

"Oh, just a little thing," Anna said. "Like me being gripped in the talons of a giant bird and flying over the forest toward certain death."

"What? Are you hurt?"

"She's okay, but she needs some of that antiseptic gel," Yoshi said. He snuck a glance at the compound, where the others were building a fire. "But, Molly, first we have to talk. We found something. Something you need to know. Somebody's been keeping track of time. Counting years, or trying to, anyway."

Quickly, Anna described the field, the robots, and the calendar someone had kept on the tree rings. She described the end flourish on the mark. "It looks just like the marks Hank made in the tuber book."

The implications clicked through Molly's mind. "That means he knows that the Cubs are caught in a time warp. Which means that—"

"We could be in one right now," Anna said. "And it might not be by accident. We don't know everything our devices are capable of. If they can warp gravity, maybe they can do the same for time."

"He doesn't want us to leave," Yoshi said. "We could be his prisoners and not even know it."

Molly dug something from her pack. It was the smartphone they'd salvaged from the luggage in the desert. "I've been saving this. It has a little battery life on it." She looked at both of them. "I have to know."

They nodded. Molly switched it on. As soon as she saw the date she powered it down again.

"How long do you think we've been here?" she asked them.

"Only a night," Anna said. "Or was it two?"

"One," Yoshi said. "I think."

"According to the phone's internal calendar, we've been here almost two days," Molly said.

"How trustworthy is that, even?" Yoshi asked. "Could the phone be fooled, too?"

"Yes," Molly said. "Which is why I'm going to activate the GPS receiver, so the phone can sync to whatever date or time it truly is."

Yoshi opened his mouth to speak, then closed it. "You— *what*? I thought we couldn't *get* any GPS signals!"

Molly sighed. "We couldn't, but I've got an idea. I think we should try the gravity device's tech-boosting setting."

Anna looked at her doubtfully. "That setting has a habit of blowing things up."

"We'll just use it for a second," Molly said. "Enough time for the phone to get a ping. It's a gamble. The boost may not even work that way. Or it could destroy the phone outright. But I think the risk is worth it."

Anna and Yoshi frowned at each other for a long moment, then Yoshi nodded and held out the ring.

"Let's be fast," he grumbled. "Get ready for bright." He twisted the ring around to the symbol they'd learned meant *tech*, and pressed the *more* glyph.

Suddenly the phone burst to life, the screen beaming like a flashlight. Molly felt it grow warm in her hand, then almost scorching hot.

"Quick! Turn it off!" she said, nearly dropping the phone.

"Going dark." Yoshi deactivated the ring.

For a moment, all Molly could do was lob the phone from hand to hand, like a one-person game of Hot Potato. "I probably shouldn't have been holding this when we tried that, huh?"

Then, when it had finally cooled, she turned the screen on again.

"Two weeks . . ." Molly rasped. "We've been here for *two whole weeks*."

Yoshi scowled and Anna covered her mouth in shock.

"We're leaving," Yoshi said. "All of us."

"But what about the others? What should we do?" Anna asked.

"We have to tell the Cubs," Molly answered. "Hank has to be stopped. He's messing with all of them."

Yoshi nodded. "I agree."

"But before I do, we have to try to convince them to come with us."

"I don't think they will," Anna said. "But even if we tell them, why would they believe us?"

Molly held up the smartphone. "I still have a tiny bit of charge yet."

"They may not trust our calendar," Anna said.

"The phone itself, though," Molly told them. "It's enough to prove we're from the future."

They joined the group around the fire. Slide-whistle birds roasted on a crude grill. Stu and Drew and Dana were on meal duty, turning tubers with sharp sticks. Kimberly had gathered plates and forks, Javi trailing behind her to help set the places, and Crash was spooning red berry jam into a bowl. Everyone had a job, everyone knew what to think and where to go. It was why the Cubs had done so well here. And she was about to throw a bomb in their midst.

Molly walked to the front of the semicircle. Everyone paused from their tasks and looked up. Hank appeared uneasy. He took a step forward, as if to try and stop her, but he halted, waiting.

"First, we all want to thank you for welcoming us and help-ing us," Molly said. "Second, we want to tell you that we're leaving tomorrow morning at first light."

"But we agreed," Hank said. "One more day."

"We're going to take our chances. Anna and Yoshi made it beyond the stream today, and they think the triple Ds—or the big beaks—are migrating out of the forest. We're going to make it to the ridge, no matter what. We're going to make it to the end of the valley, and we're going to find answers there. We want you all to come with us. There's strength in num-bers, and we could use all your skills."

"Abandon the compound?" Kimberly asked. "That doesn't make sense. We worked so hard. We'll get rescued eventually."

"Leaving is the right thing to do," Anna said. "You have to trust us."

"But you don't know any more than we do, really," Kimberly said. "I mean, no offense—*none* of us really know much. We're all guessing. You saw a diagram of a thing you can't identify at the end of the valley. That's it. You don't know what it is, or why it's there, or if it can help us. You listened to your friend, who might be under a spell or a truth serum or something. He said there was help for someone like Cal. But what's the proof?"

"How do you know about Oliver?" Molly asked.

Kimberly hesitated. She looked at Hank.

"I told her," Hank said gruffly. "I tell them everything."

"Everything?" Molly asked sharply. Hank looked away.

"My point is," Kimberly said, recovering, "you could be heading into *worse* danger."

Pammy nodded. "We lost so many people already."

"Listen, I'm all for bashing through the defensive line for a touchdown," Crash said, "but only if I have a good chance of reaching the fifty-yard line."

"We figured out how to stay alive," Dana said. "I'm sure that planes are still searching. And even if they'd given up on us, now they'll be looking for you!"

Molly looked at the Killbots. Javi silently shook his head. But Yoshi and Anna both nodded. Kira and Akiko seemed like they knew what she was about to say, too. She saw sympathy in their gazes.

"There's something you don't know," she said. She took a deep breath. "Hank *doesn't* tell you everything."

24

Javi

o! Don't do it, Molly, don't tell them . . .

"You've been here longer than you think," Molly said.

"How much longer?" Kimberly asked.

Javi bored into her with his eyes. He *willed* her not to say any more. But she wouldn't make eye contact with him.

"Over fifty years," Molly said.

Kimberly laughed out loud. "Sure. And I'm a grandma."

"Well, your mother probably is," Anna said.

Molly shot Anna a warning look. Javi knew that look. It meant, *Let me handle this.*

"What are you talking about?" Dana asked. "Hank?" She looked at him for answers, and he shook his head and glanced at the ground.

Javi saw the fear and confusion on her face, and he looked away, too.

"Listen, you're in some kind of . . . a time-distortion field," Molly said. "It seems like it's just here, in the woods. It ends at the stream, we think."

"A time . . . what?" Dana echoed.

Yoshi cleared his throat. "She means that time is moving differently in the forest. Outside, fifty years have passed while you've been here in your compound."

"This sounds like bunk. How would that even be possible?" Crash asked. He looked around at his friends. "We look the same as we did when we got here."

"We don't know how it works, exactly," Anna said. "All I know is that lots of the science stuff we learned in school functions *differently* here. Gravity and nature are all screwed up—why can't time be screwy, too?"

"Think about it . . . " Javi said weakly. Now that the cat was out of the bag, he couldn't just let Molly flounder. Or the Cub-Tones. "Doesn't time feel strange here? Don't you lose track of it, the way some days are long, like when you're in school, and some days are short, like summer vacation? Or how long the car ride is to the beach, but how short it feels coming home? But hey, you're still the same age at the end of the year, right?"

"That doesn't explain fifty years passing in a couple of months, dad," Crash said. "You can't noodle that out."

"Sure we can," Yoshi said impatiently. "We're from the future. To bend time you just go to a Starbucks, activate a venti, and hyperlink into a Prius. We do it all the time."

"Yoshi," Molly chided. "Can you please cut it out? Look, we know this is a lot to absorb."

"I don't believe you," Pammy said. Her voice shook.

"Theories," Crash said. "That and a quarter will buy me a loaf of bread."

"Not anymore," Yoshi said.

"Let me get this straight," Dana said. "You're really from . . . the future?"

"Did you crash your spaceship?" Stu asked in a teasing voice.

"No, we came on a plane, just like you," Molly said. "And we're not from the future . . . We're from the present."

"I'm so confused," Kimberly said.

Molly held up her smartphone. "But we have these. This is a phone that runs on a battery. But it's also a computer."

"Computers are big," Stu said. "That's impossible."

"I can get movies and TV and music on it," Molly continued.

Javi looked at the faces of the Cubs. They were disbelieving, but . . . fascinated.

"I can play games on it, and I can send messages, and I can access search engines. That means that if I type in a topic, in seconds I'll find out everything about it. If I typed in *Bear Claw*, I'd have a map of where it is, directions on how to get there, what the population is, and the best place to eat breakfast on Sundays."

"Like fun you can!" Crash exploded. "Is it April Fools'? Is that it?"

"So show us, if you're telling the truth," Kimberly said. Her voice was quiet.

"I only have a little bit of battery life," Molly said. "And obviously I can't get a signal to communicate with the outside world. Phones connect to satellites, but you have to be within the network."

"Well, that makes no sense at all," Crash said. "Phones connect to wires. Everybody knows that."

"How does it work?" Dana asked.

"It connects to a tractor beam on Tatooine," Yoshi said. "Then it's rerouted through the Pilates system."

"Cut it out!" Molly snapped. "This is hard enough for them, Yoshi!"

"So stop hesitating. Just turn on the phone and show them," Yoshi said. "Compassion is a swift sword. Do it!"

"No!" Pammy leaped back. She looked at the others frantically, whipping her head around. "What if that's some sort of Commie device? From Russia or Red China?"

"Actually, it *was* manufactured in China—" Anna started, but Molly shot her a furious look.

Molly held up a hand. She turned on the phone. Javi thought she might access the photos, but of course she didn't. That would have felt wrong—like a violation. He peeked over her shoulder as she opened the music, scrolling quickly through the list of songs until she found one she wanted to play. Despite the seriousness of the moment, she made a small smile when she tapped the screen.

It was like getting smacked over the head. Javi knew immediately what Molly had chosen. It was "Up on the Roof," a song the two of them had sung together once at a school talent show on a dare. An old song about leaving the world behind.

They hadn't done very well. Singing, it had turned out, was not among their talents. But it had still been an amazing night.

"I know that song," Kimberly said. She took the phone and stared at it. There was a screen saver of twisting, pulsating multicolored lights playing across the screen.

"What . . . is this?" Dana looked over Kimberly's shoulder.

Kimberly silently passed the phone to Dana, who passed it to Crash, who passed it along the line. Pammy refused to touch it but couldn't resist looking at it.

Javi closed his eyes when the music abruptly cut out. The battery was dead. It felt like losing another link home. He thought of their own phones, lost in the exploding plane. They had held pictures of parents, homes, streets, cupcakes, birthday cakes, beaches, parks. Favorite songs. Old texts. Gone forever now.

Dana reached for Kimberly's hand. She looked shaken. "If this is true . . . nobody's looking for us anymore."

"No," Molly said. "But if it helps, I don't think anybody is looking for us, either."

"Fifty years," Pammy said. "That means that . . . my big brother is older than my dad!"

"No, he isn't," Dana said quietly. "It means your father is as old as your grandfather."

"If he's still alive," Anna pointed out. At Molly's look, she added quickly, "I mean, of course he is, I'm just saying . . . the world is, you know, different." As Pammy began to cry, she added, "Life spans are even longer now, especially if you don't smoke."

Javi's gaze went from one face to another. He saw it happen before his eyes, each one of them absorbing the news, thinking about their parents, their siblings, their grandparents, their teachers, their pets . . . Everything they had, everything they wanted to get back to, was gone or completely different, as though they were now strangers in the world.

Every face. Except Hank's.

"Why did you tell them?" Hank cried. "I told you this would happen!"

"What do you mean?" Kimberly asked. "You *knew*?"

"Molly told me earlier today," he said.

"We think you knew earlier than that," Molly said.

Javi had to admire the way Hank took his time answering Molly's challenge. There were no heated denials. He seemed to think through his options before speaking. "Why would I tell them? Look at them now. Are they better off?"

"Because we needed to know!" Kimberly burst out.

"Because we deserved to know," Dana said.

"I don't want to know," Pammy said, sobbing. "I wish I didn't! I miss my mom!"

Everyone went silent for a moment. Kimberly slipped her arm around Pammy and drew her close.

Molly's eyes glinted in the firelight. Javi knew that look. She was zeroing in on Hank. She was about to hit him with some truth. "There's a fallen tree in the forest," she said. "One of the ones that grow upside down so the roots are exposed. It's marked—someone was using it like a calendar. Trying to count the years."

The Cubs all turned to look at their leader.

"Hank?" Kimberly questioned. "What is she talking about?"

"How did you do it, Hank?" Molly asked. "How did you make the time warp? Is it the device?"

"Stop accusing me! I didn't do anything wrong!" Hank spit out the words.

"You did," Molly said. "You knew that time was advancing. How could you know that if you weren't *doing* it? You're the one who created the time warp. How?"

"Don't listen to them. Kim! Crash! Stu . . . "

They all shook their heads at him. Kimberly turned away.

Dana stood. "We need answers."

"Answers?" Hank chuckled hollowly. "That's a laugh! You didn't want to know! I'm the one who went beyond the stream, who saw a creature almost rip my best friend's face off. I was the one who dragged him back *alone*. All you needed was to feel safe. I protected you!"

"No!" Dana shouted. "We protected each other! *What did you do to us?*"

Hank's lips pressed together.

"You're no leader," Crash said. "You're just a rat fink."

"Search him," Dana said.

25

Yoshi

Yoshi crossed to Hank. "Turn out your pockets."

"Kim? Crash? Go through his lean-to," Dana said.

Hank turned out his pockets. They were full of holes. He couldn't hide anything in them anyway.

Pammy was still sobbing, and it was distracting. If Hank was manipulating time, they needed answers fast. Yoshi felt his own panic race through him, and he turned angrily. "Will you please put a sock in it?"

"Yoshi-chan!" Akiko spoke to him sharply in Japanese. "Would you put yourself in her place right now?"

"If I were in her place, I'd suck it up!"

"If you were in her place and were filled with grief, we would try to comfort you."

The remark stung. She was chiding him. Warning him

about his lack of *omoiyari*—compassion and sensitivity to the needs of others.

He touched his katana for reassurance. It made him feel strong. Not at the mercy of emotions the way Pammy was. What did Akiko expect from him?

But how would he feel, knowing the world was fifty years ahead of when he left it? That it had continued to spin past days and weeks and years without him in it? It had to be about the loneliest feeling imaginable.

Was he just a frog in a well? Not seeing the whole picture, not understanding how shocked the Cubs must feel?

"Nothing in the lean-to," Crash called.

Omoiyari. And Anna's words in his head. "Don't you ever just *talk* to people?"

Yoshi glanced at Hank. This time he really looked at Hank, past his defiance into his panic. And his sense of responsibility for the Cub-Tones.

"Hank, listen," Yoshi said. "This place is hard on all of us. I'm guessing whatever you did, you did it to protect your people. Tell us how it works. We all want the same thing. To get home."

Hank took a deep breath. Like he was in a witness box about to testify, Yoshi thought. Why not? They were all facing him now, like a jury.

"We were hungry," Hank said. He turned to face the Cubs. "Do you remember? Day after day, it got worse. The plane food ran out fast, before it even occurred to us that we should be rationing it. We thought we'd be rescued within days, remember? We couldn't manage to catch the slide-whistle birds. We didn't have a sword, or even a sharp knife. And water . . . The stream kept *moving*. Some days we couldn't find it at all. We couldn't get enough water, so we had to ration it. Every time we tried to hike out, we got lost, or attacked. It was . . . chaos. We lost five of our friends in the first two weeks. Five! We ate bugs and berries, and we were getting weaker by the day."

"It was hard," Dana said, her voice curt. "But it doesn't justify—"

Hank interrupted her. "Then we found the tubers. They could be our main food source. The only problem was the long growing cycle. I grew up on a farm, and I know crop yields. The tubers grew so slowly . . . We'd run out. We'd starve. So Cal and I volunteered to leave. To go beyond the stream, look for new food sources. And you would have two fewer mouths to feed for a while. That was the trip when he was attacked. But before that . . . we came to this clearing. There were all these rusting metal parts."

"They were robots," Yoshi said. "Anna and I saw them."

"That's when we really knew that things were . . . seriously weird," Hank said. "That it was no ordinary plane crash. And it's where I found both devices. I mean, not just the water-changer that looks like your device, but the time-changer. We had no idea what they were. We just put them in our pockets. They just seemed like strange tools. We kept walking and we got lost. Again. We stumbled onto that grove of the upside-down trees. Cal noticed the broken ones all had the same number of rings. The fat trees, the skinny trees, tall or short . . . they were all exactly the same age. He said that was strange. He was smart about that kind of stuff."

"It's another sign this place is engineered," Anna said. "It's not really a natural environment at all."

"Yeah, he said something like that, too. Anyway, I put a notch in one of the trunks, so we could come back and keep track of time. It seemed important. Then the jawbugs attacked, and we ran . . . right into a big beak." He looked at Molly. "Well, you all know how awful that is."

"Go on," Molly said.

"We barely got away. In the panic, I forgot all about the devices. We made it back to the compound, but Cal almost died." He stopped.

Akiko and Kira looked at Yoshi for a translation. Yoshi told them quickly, this time not leaving things out because he was bored or didn't really care. As Hank spoke again, he would pause so that Yoshi could translate.

"I thought we were gone three days. It was three weeks. That was a surprise, but I just figured that shock had sort of unhinged us or something. The others were in rough shape. The tubers had run out. I'd lost my device—had a hole in my pocket—but Cal still had his. Dana, you remember, you were helping me figure out the indicators and then we twisted the thing and just found out by accident—"

"That it turned the water into a gel," Dana said. "The water pitcher just transformed before our eyes. We couldn't believe it."

"We could store water! And heat! And I thought—if this did that, what could the other one do? I searched and searched, and finally found it in the patch of wild tubers. They were fully grown! It was amazing. I realized that it had something to do with time. So I experimented with the symbols. There was no way to track how much time had passed except by the size of the tubers. That's why I kept such detailed notes on them."

"So you kept doing it," Molly said.

"We always had enough food if I moved time a few weeks or months ahead," Hank said. "I figured out how to measure out the time on the device."

"Why didn't you tell us?" Dana asked. "It should have been a group decision!"

"At first I just thought I'd try it, see if it worked," Hank said. "I didn't want to scare anybody. And then, I thought . . . well, I pretty much had given up on search planes by that point. There were two things that could happen. One, we'd just live here until . . . well, until either we were killed, or we died of old age. Two, eventually technology would change enough, maybe better radar or something, better planes, and we'd get rescued. If time moved forward, that would better our chances. I broke my watch so that we couldn't use it, but when I moved the indicator on the device I'd slip back to the tree so I could keep a record. It was hard to keep track, though. I think the device is imprecise, or the time folds it makes are unpredictable. There are places in the woods that warp time. Sometimes I'd get lost and not know how long had passed."

"I saw distortions when I was above the forest," Anna said. "I think they could be time folds. It's like the heavy gravity ring that killed Caleb, or the cloaked barriers in the desert. They seemed to correspond to the trees with the misshapen trunks."

"None of this explains why you moved us fifty years ahead!" Kimberly cried. "It's horrible! I don't want to be in the future!"

"I didn't know!" Hank insisted. "When Molly told me fifty years had passed I couldn't believe it! I thought it might have been a *few years*, five or six at the most. Obviously, I messed up somehow. But we stayed alive."

"That doesn't explain why you tried to trap us with you," Yoshi said.

"What?" Hank asked.

"We thought we were here two days and it's been over two weeks," Molly said.

"You . . . trick us," Kira said, her eyes narrowed.

"And by the way," Yoshi said, "the Beatles broke up."

"I didn't do it!" Hank insisted. "I wouldn't trap you here. I wanted you to stay, sure. We could use your skills. You probably know things from the future that could help us. But I wouldn't trap you!" Hank made an impatient gesture. "I wish I'd never found that device."

"The Beatles broke up?" Pammy moaned. "Could things get any worse?"

"If I've learned anything in this place," Crash mumbled, "it's that the answer to that question is always yes."

"Can we see the device?" Javi asked Hank. "You said it didn't look like the others."

Hank reached into his oboe case. He held out a small metal object.

Yoshi peered at it. "I've seen this before," he said.

26

Anna

Anna turned the device over in her hands. She looked up at Yoshi. "The jawbug nest."

"Same shape, right?" Yoshi asked.

She nodded. "Exactly the same. But . . . why? This is crazy. Why should the timey-wimey device be part of an insect nest?"

"Maybe it isn't a real nest," Yoshi said. "We didn't truly examine it. Why would we? Who would pick up a wasp nest?"

"Of course . . . " Anna said. "The metallic sound. The nests are made of metal. And there were dozens of them in that grove where you killed the snakehog."

"And covering that cave opening," Yoshi said.

"Wait a second," Hank said. "There's a cave?"

Yoshi nodded. "I saw it. It's deep in the grove."

"Okay, theories?" Molly asked. "Because if the nests aren't nests, then maybe that means the jawbugs aren't bugs."

"What else could they possibly be?" Kimberly asked.

"Robots," the Killbots all said together.

"Maybe the jawbugs don't just attack because they're guarding their nest," Anna said. "If they're machines like the ones we've seen, they could be protecting something else."

"What are they protecting?" Molly asked as Yoshi translated for the sisters. "Theories? Conjectures?"

"Another pod like the one in the desert?" Javi suggested.

"Or some larger piece of machinery," Anna said. "When I was above the trees, I thought I saw the time folds radiating out from a central spot. They looked like spokes on a wheel. I saw . . . something in the middle. I think it was the glint of metal. Kira said there are no rock formations in the forest."

"There's also the apex predator," Yoshi said. "I think it lives in the cave. Anna and I could feel the vibration of something moving below the ground."

"The Thing," Dana said.

"So, we should never go there, right?" Pammy put in with a nervous smile.

Molly whistled. "If the Thing is living in that cave with the jawbugs, it could be more intelligent than we realized," she said. "Maybe it's not a simple predator. Maybe it *is* like the pod Javi saw in the desert. *Maybe* it's part of whatever alien species built this place."

"Wait a second," Crash said. "Have you flipped your lid?"

"You mean, like Martians?" Stu asked.

"We don't know what planet," Anna said. "But it's unlikely

to be Mars. There's no life there. At least not anymore. Let's stick to the facts."

"Creatures from another planet are *facts*?" Drew asked, his mouth open in disbelief.

"Not necessarily a planet from our solar system," Anna said. "Could even be from another galaxy. But there's something else . . . " Anna pulled a loose strand of hair behind her ear. "Another element that doesn't quite add up. Yoshi and I found that field Hank mentioned. It was full of destroyed worker robots, the kind we've seen everywhere. To be honest, it looked like a battlefield. Some thing—or things—had gathered them there to be destroyed."

Molly frowned. "That doesn't make sense. The worker robots maintain the rift and everything in it. Why would something do that, especially if it's a part of all this?"

"Weirdsmobile," Crash agreed. "Like, we find devices that help us survive, and yet the whole forest is trying to kill us. This is not consistent with my general world view, dad. Are we dealing with friends or enemies? I'd just like to know."

"It's not that simple," said Anna.

"Why not?" Dana asked quietly. "Crash could be onto something. What if there are *two* forces at work?" She glanced from Javi to Anna to Yoshi, her eyes finally landing on Molly. "There's the something that brought us here and wants us to find whatever's at the end of the rift—and the something that wants to keep us from it. Maybe even trap us in time."

Molly opened her mouth to respond but stopped, her expression thoughtful. Her eyes found Anna's.

"We just always assumed the robots were on the same side . . . " Anna muttered.

"And it fits our theory," Kimberly said cheerily. "The Commies versus the Red, White, and Blue!"

Anna thought back to how they'd arrived—how on the plane she'd felt chosen to survive—and how the devices helped them while the environment tried to hurt them. Hadn't the pincer bots and the workers been at odds occasionally?

"So, what do we do?" Hank asked.

Molly sighed, running a hand over her face. "These are interesting theories, but for now that's all they are. Before we do anything, I'd like to try to get through to Cal. Earlier, he had me put my hands on the ground. He wanted me to feel something."

"I'm feeling something right now," Javi said. "Confused."

"He could know something we don't, is my point," Molly said.

"He's over by the fire," Dana said. She looked over Anna's shoulder. Then her eyes suddenly widened in alarm. "Cal, NO!" she shouted.

27

Javi

Cal stood by the table, holding Hank's reeds in his hands. Javi could see his green rash pulsing in the gray light.

"Two five six!" he shouted.

Hank ran across the compound. "No, Cal!"

He held the reeds high.

Hank stopped a foot away. "Please. Don't do it." His voice broke. "Those are my last reeds. I can't play without them. You *know* that."

Cal broke the reeds in half and threw them in the air. Then he reached for Hank's oboe. He held it in his hands as though he'd never seen an instrument before. Like a stick he was about to snap. "Frequency sequence!" he shouted.

"Stop!" Dana and Hank shouted the word at the same time. They launched themselves at Cal, but he twisted away. The more they tried to hold him, the more violently he resisted. He put his mouth on the oboe and blew. A discordant note bleated out, then slid wildly from one pitch to another.

There was something about their desperation and that sound that almost tore Javi's heart out. "We have to do something," he said to Molly.

But Molly had a strange expression on her face as Cal blew into the oboe again. "I'm starting to get it," she said.

"Get what?"

"Sounds, words," she said. "Scraps of meaning."

"I don't know what you're talking about."

Javi looked from Molly's rapt expression to the writhing Cal, who was now crouching over the instrument as he tried to hold off Hank. The sounds changed, becoming short and fast.

The blue cubes flickered and went out.

"STOP!" Molly shouted, and Dana and Hank looked over at her, surprised.

"Cal just did that," she said. "He turned out the lights in the gel cube. With the oboe. It's a sound that said 'off.' I *heard* it."

Hank looked from the oboe to the gel cubes.

"Play, Cal," Molly said. "Do it again."

Cal blew into the oboe. The lights in the cubes flared.

"Don't you see? There's a *reason* he broke the reeds and tried to alter Dana's flute," Molly said. "He's losing our language but he's gaining another at the same time. He wants to be able to tell you."

"Tell us what?" Hank asked.

Molly ran her hands through her hair. "I don't know. I just know he's trying to communicate. Do you remember when you were playing that weird music with Akiko? All those funny notes?"

"Actually, it was a series of glissandos. You glide from one pitch to another—"

"Whatever! The light in the cubes flickered. You were controlling it, you just didn't know it. And all those times you tried to play with the reeds that didn't work?"

"I did it at night so I didn't drive everyone crazy."

"But it was right outside Cal's hut! He could hear it!"

"Sometimes it would calm him down . . . "

"Maybe because he thought you were trying to understand the language."

"Sometimes it would agitate him."

"Because you were getting it wrong! Don't you see? He always *reacted*. Maybe he was trying to stop you! What if you were turning up the time sometimes, by mistake? If sound can affect the technology here, you could have been doing it without realizing."

Hank looked stricken. "I hope not. That means . . . that means it *is* my fault."

"Well, of course it's your fault," Anna said. Javi nudged her. "I mean, technically. You kept the time-changer a secret."

Kira was flipping through her sketchbook excitedly. She brought it over to Molly and pointed to a drawing. She had sketched the Cubs' and Killbots' devices side by side. She pointed to the markings that ran along the outside of the devices, markings they had never quite figured out.

"Scale," Akiko said.

Kira nodded. She handed her pencil to Akiko, who placed a treble clef on the lines.

"A musical staff," Hank said. "The indicator lights line up like notes."

"Music," Akiko said.

"Exactly." Hank turned excitedly to Cal, now sitting on the ground. "That's what you were trying to say! It's not a chromatic or a diatonic scale. It's not music that's pleasant to our ears, but it's mathematical, just like our music is."

"Ratio," Cal said.

"The numbers!" Dana cried. "Four, five, six."

"Why didn't I get it?" Hank thumped his head. "Major chord!"

"Can you translate for the nonmusical here?" Molly asked.

"What's the difference between music and noise?" Hank asked.

"Um, music sounds good?" Javi suggested.

"Exactly. It's all about tones. If the sound waves produce an irregular vibration, we hear it as noise. Notes vibrate at certain ratios. Like major chords. A four, five, six ratio makes a major chord."

"Four five six is not the ratio," Cal repeated.

"I always thought that we could express anything in music with the notes that we have," Hank went on. "But what if there are *other* kinds of scales that communicate? That would create different vibrations, different harmonies!" He turned to Molly. "Remember what you said about the 'multiverse'? This is the same thing. It's a whole different dimension of sound."

"But if it's not a kind of scale you know, how can you translate it?" Javi asked.

Hank tapped Kira's sketchbook. "There's got to be a marker," he said. "Like middle C. Something that makes sense of the scale. So, we can *communicate*. We could decode the language. We could talk to Cal!"

Cal began to play the oboe again. Instead of the sweet, mournful sound, something else emerged, some kind of noise that was urgent and precise. Javi saw the musicians in the group wince, but he could tell they were trying to pick out notes. Something to decipher in their language of music.

Molly, though—she could hear it. He saw her chin lift, and something flashed in her eyes he'd never seen before. It scared him, but it thrilled him, too. Something powerful, something . . . beyond.

"'Breakdown'!" she cried. "That's the meaning the sound is making!"

"What does that mean?" Javi asked her.

With a sudden movement that felt like a huge exhalation of breath, birds left the trees and took to the sky. For a moment the sky was so covered with birds that it was as dark as night.

A moment later they were gone.

Now they could hear the eerie silence of the forest. No birds twittered. No leaf stirred.

Cal blew into the oboe again. The sound seemed to pierce Molly. She jerked backward. The word that came rushing out seemed to surprise her as much as them.

"'Danger,'" she said.

Anna broke the silence. "We've been in danger since we got here."

"This is different," Molly said. She beat her fist against her leg. "It's like I'm only hearing static. A word might break free, but . . . I can't understand the whole. But it feels very urgent. I don't have time to decipher it! The only one who can help us is Cal." She bent down next to him. "Cal, you have to try. You have to remember your old language. *Our* language. You can't let it go!" She looked up at Hank. "Give him a memory."

"What kind of memory?"

"Anything! Good, bad, everyday ordinary; perfect, spectacular, horrible, terrible—"

"Okay!" Hank crouched down near Cal. "We were eleven, maybe twelve? You were helping me with a chore. Painting the garden fence for my mom. Remember? It was a heat wave in August. We were halfway done and just about ready to quit, except we knew my dad wouldn't let us. Then he drove up in the truck and said, 'Hey, boys, you wouldn't want to go to the lake right now, would you?' We jumped in the truck and then swam all afternoon. It was the best day."

Cal's face was a blank.

"Your mom's peach ice cream," Hank said, desperation in his voice. "Or the time we snuck out that summer night and ran through town at midnight and Garvin Tyler saw us and told on us. That time you threw a baseball out the window during class, just so you'd get detention with me. The way your mom would say *Calvin Emerson Tapper*, and that's when you knew you were in trouble . . . " Hank stopped as Cal's face stayed completely blank. "It's no use, Molly. He's gone."

"He's not gone if he's still here," Javi said fiercely. "Let me try." He crouched on the ground next to Cal. "You've got to remember what you lost, pal. Friendship."

"Please," Cal said in a small voice. "Hurts."

"Copy that," Javi said. "Life hurts. Especially here. But look, if you can forget about the almost-getting-killed stuff, and the total lack of cheeseburgers, you have to admit this is cool. We're figuring this place out, one step at a time. Together."

"Frequency sequence."

"I get it. Sounds are becoming your language. Molly explained. But you still have words inside you. We just need more of them. And you're still Hank's best friend, dude." Javi looked into Cal's face, trying to break through the blankness. "It's hard to remember ice cream when you can't get any. But if we lose that memory—of cold and sweet—if we lose what made us happy, then we lose, *period*."

"Bad good," Cal said.

"Everyday, ordinary, perfect, spectacular," Molly said. "Horrible, terrible. All of it."

Cal struggled to speak. "Strawberry peach!" he burst out.

"That's right, buddy," Hank said softly. "That's your favorite. I forgot. She made it for your birthday."

"Intruder," he said.

"No, Cal," Hank said, frustrated. "Molly isn't—"

"Not her," Cal said. "The battle. Ambush. Two forces. Robots destroyed."

"The battlefield," Yoshi said.

"The Intruder tried a takeover. Maintenance is in damage mode." He gazed at Molly, and Javi could see something human reach out to her. "You said there was help."

"We think so," Molly said. "We hope so. Do you . . . ever see a building?"

"Like a tower. Bigger than a ship. It comes in dreams."

"Yes."

"I need to get there."

"Of course," Hank said. "Of course, we'll all get you there.

Together we can make it." He looked up at the Cubs. "We're going to get to the ridge and we're going to keep on going."

"Of course," Dana said, and the others joined in.

"We stick," Hank said.

Cal almost smiled. He struggled to get out the words. "Like . . . glue."

Molly

The Killbots were packed and ready in minutes. They followed behind the Cubs, helping to gather supplies. They packed water gel cubes, dried fruit, seed cakes, and as many tubers as they could carry. Dana brought the first aid kit she'd assembled. They rolled up blankets and tied them to backpacks.

"Everyone ready?" Hank called as they assembled in the middle of the compound. The eyes of all the Cubs were on the musical instruments left on the long table.

The flute, the oboe, and the piccolo weren't a problem. They were light and easily carried. But when it came to essential items, would a French horn, a saxophone, a trumpet, and cymbals qualify?

Crash put his hand on his glockenspiel. "Good-bye, pal."

Stu patted his saxophone. Drew put his French horn next to it. Pammy cradled her trumpet. They all looked as though they might cry.

Molly understood. Music had kept them together and kept them going.

"I don't think there's anything funny about a glockenspiel anymore," Javi said.

"Thanks, little buddy," Crash said.

Hank and Yoshi took the lead. Molly hung back. She touched Javi's arm as he trudged up, shouldering his pack. "Walk with me?"

"Sure."

They walked in silence. Their strides still fit because Javi made his longer and she made hers shorter. They weren't even conscious of it, really. It just happened.

As they walked deeper into the forest, the mist seemed to sweep around them like a curtain. Molly could feel cold droplets on her hair and skin. The others were just shapes moving ahead of them in the shadows.

"I'm sorry for what I said yesterday . . . or was it last week?" Javi gave Molly a rueful grin. "I don't blame you about Oliver. I really don't."

"Thanks." Molly's fingers went to the ridge on her shoulder.

"I don't know why I said it. I—"

"It's okay. I get it. Sometimes when we're scared we say the wrong thing. I do it all the time, and I'm more scared now than I think I've ever been." Molly grimaced. "Javi, something's happening to me. Because of the bite."

"I know." He turned to her, warm eyes concerned. "Does it hurt?"

"It's not that. It's what it's doing to me. I'm becoming . . . not me. I'm changing into something else. It's why I can understand Cal. Cal said I was letting go of being human. I'm becoming like him."

"Yeah, I figured that out," Javi said.

"I'm scared," she whispered.

"I am, too," Javi said.

"What should I do?" Molly asked. She winced when she heard the pleading note in her own voice. There was a difference between asking people for conjectures and theories and asking them for help. She wasn't used to it.

Javi was quiet. They walked down the path as the leaves shivered with a chilly wind.

"Okay," he said finally, and suddenly she felt a flood of gratitude for her friend. Deep and warm. It was how he'd been when her father was dying. She'd tell him the worst news, the saddest things, and he'd just . . . absorb it. Then he'd say, "Okay." And that meant, just . . . okay. He got it. He'd carry it along with her. *Bad things happen. I'm still here and so are you.* That had pulled her through everything.

But this . . . could it pull her through this?

"There's nothing you *can* do, so we just have to keep going," he said. "Every time we apply logic to this place, what we think falls apart, right? So we can't really *know* anything. Maybe isolating Cal like the Cubs did was a huge mistake. Maybe they should have been less afraid. Figured out a different way. Maybe the time jumps made it worse. We really don't know. We can't trust gravity here, or time. But I know this—we can trust each other. We're going to hang on to Molly, okay? No matter what."

She felt Javi grip her hand.

"I won't let you go," he said.

Molly took a deep breath. "Okay," she said.

Yoshi

Yoshi looked behind him. Molly and Javi were yards away. Stu and Drew and Pammy were dragging, their heads together in close conversation. Dana trailed behind with Cal. He wished they'd hurry.

Other people. Always messing with your speed.

"Pammy is scared to come," Hank said from beside him. "I know it seems like she's a nuisance, but she's actually the one who figured out how to make those seed cakes and set up the lean-tos. We wouldn't have survived without her. Kimberly seems like she lives in a pep rally, but she's super smart and keeps our spirits up. Crash is really strong, and he'll keep going until he drops. Stu and Drew . . . they're not leaders, sure, but they'll do anything for the team. And Dana was the smartest kid in our school. I depend on her. We're not just a burden."

"I didn't think you were," Yoshi said.

Hank grinned. "Are you kidding? It's written all over your face. It's okay. I made a lot of mistakes. One of them was with Cal. I thought he was unpredictable. I thought he would smash things or get violent. I should have figured it out. Just because you can't predict what he'll do doesn't mean he's unpredictable."

"That doesn't make sense," Yoshi said. He wanted to sound gruff, but instead he sounded curious. Probably because he was.

"We just had to figure out what he was trying to say," Hank said. "Molly saw that. Just because I couldn't understand his words, doesn't mean they were meaningless."

"Molly was bitten by a triple D, too," Yoshi said. "She's lucky the attack wasn't worse. She's healed completely."

Hank bit his lip and looked away, as if searching for predators. "Right. She's lucky."

"Shouldn't we be at the stream by now?" Yoshi asked.

Hank frowned. "Yes. It's always hard to tell, but we've been walking for a while. It must have changed course again."

Yoshi looked down at his feet. The ground felt spongy. He knelt down and put his hand on the wet earth. "It didn't change course," he said. "It disappeared. I think the stream dried up. Or moved underground."

"That's good news, right? We can just head to the ridge."

"Maybe," Yoshi said. Something was bothering him. He

squinted ahead. The mist was turning to sleet. It was the coldest he'd ever felt here. He waited until the others caught up. "Molly? It's hard to tell, but I think I see—"

"Distortion," Molly said. "I see it, too. There's a time fold ahead of us."

Yoshi felt the ground lurch. Somewhere deep in the woods a tree fell, its sound a violent cracking that made everyone jump.

Now they could feel it underneath their feet. The ground was vibrating, sometimes heaving in great jerks. Every few moments another tree would crash in the forest.

Then, ahead in the distortion field, the sleet suddenly hung in the air, as if it had frozen there.

"What . . . is that?" Dana said. She reached out her hand as if to touch it, but Yoshi grabbed her wrist.

"I wouldn't do that if I were you," he said. "I think time just stopped in there."

"Maintenance is in damage mode," Cal said. "We're breaking up. We have to restore!"

"Restore what?" Hank asked him.

"It can't execute the code!"

Suddenly, Cal broke away from the group. He plunged wildly into the forest.

The Cubs and the Killbots dashed after him, leaping over fallen branches and wet leaves, weaving through the trees. He disappeared in the cold gray mist.

"Cal!" Dana called despairingly.

"I know where he's going," Molly said, panting.

"The cave," Yoshi guessed.

Molly nodded. "You're going to meet the apex predator after all."

30

Anna

They caught up to Cal outside the upside-down tree grove. He had waited patiently for them.

"See anything?" Anna asked Molly.

Molly wiped the cold mist out of her eyes. "No distortions. I don't think it's a time fold anymore."

"No time," Cal said.

A jawbug flew out of the cave and zigzagged through the trees, heading toward them.

"It's a scout," Anna said. They stood at the edge of the time-suck grove, while the wind whistled and the trees groaned.

Another emerged and buzzed up high. Then another.

"We'd better do something soon," Yoshi said, his katana held in attack position.

"I hope you're right about the jawbugs being robots," Hank said.

The jawbug buzzed closer, and Yoshi sliced it cleanly in half with what looked like a simple flick of his sword. He kicked at the metal and wiring that spilled out. "There's your answer."

Suddenly, a great cloud of jawbugs emerged from the cave, filling the trees with a hum that Anna felt in her teeth. Beside her, Yoshi lifted his sword, glaring at the swarm.

"Wait." Hank handed his oboe to Cal. "Play the frequency," he said.

Cal put his mouth on the oboe. The sound that emerged made them jump, more a screech of a bird or a wounded animal. Not music. Not noise. The sound traveled up and down and looped in and out. It had a pattern, somehow.

The bugs circled, curling through the air like water spiraling in a whirlpool, then flew back in the cave.

Anna let out a breath. "That was amazing," she said. "So the music really does control them."

"Don't get too relieved," Molly said. "There's still the Thing in there."

Cal walked into the grove. Now Anna could see the cave opening, obscured by the thick, twisted roots. It had a dull, metallic shine.

Cal disappeared into the mouth of the cave.

"Let's go," Yoshi said, following.

Anna followed after Yoshi. He held his sword in a way that might seem casual, but Anna knew by now it was in readiness for a lightning strike. She shivered. The temperature seemed to be dropping fast. Hank held up one of the blue gels, and the light flickered on the walls. White-leafed branches snaked through the cave ceiling, looking like ghosts frozen in twisted positions. The cave walls were studded with interlocking nests, stretching one by one all the way back into darkness. Thousands and thousands of nests.

"This is spooky," Pammy whispered. "Are the jawbugs in there?"

"Probably," Anna said. "Let's hope they stay put. Because in this confined space, we'd be chomped to bits in minutes."

"Golly, thanks," Pammy said. "You're a real cheerer-upper."

"Sorry," Anna said. "I get that a lot."

The floor of the cave was smooth and flat. Icy water dripped from the ceiling. The blue light drew Anna onward. There was an ominous silence only broken by the *drip, drip* of water and their footsteps.

"You're right," she whispered to Pammy. "It is spooky." She was rewarded with a nervous smile. She was learning.

As Yoshi disappeared into the darkness, Anna suddenly realized why he'd been angry with her in the forest. It wasn't because she'd talked to Kira about him. It was because she'd thought he'd take the device when he left. She remembered when they returned, how Molly had said matter-of-factly that she knew he was coming back, because he'd taken it with him. Molly had demonstrated faith in him that Anna didn't have. What kind of a friend was she?

Oh, Anna thought. *It's the purple polka dots all over again.*

This was worse, of course. She should have trusted him.

Apparently she was learning, but not fast enough.

"Yoshi!" she called, but he was swallowed up by the darkness, following quickly on Cal's heels.

"Um," Pammy said. "Is the water getting deeper?"

"I think so," Stu said. "Don't worry, Pammy. We're going to get out of here."

"Even if we have to swim," Drew said.

"I can't swim," Pammy said.

Anna looked back at the mouth of the cave. Was water coming in? That didn't make sense. But Pammy was right. The water was lapping at her shoes. Where was it coming from? It seemed to be flowing in from one of the passageways she could see on either side of them.

They splashed through the water, hurrying after Cal and Yoshi. The cave sloped downward, twisting and turning.

Anna felt a rumble underneath her feet, and suddenly she was pitched sideways. She grabbed on to Pammy. Her hand was so cold.

"There's frost on the tree branches," Anna said. "It's getting colder by the second."

They heard a loud cracking sound, and a fissure opened up in the cave floor under their feet. They jumped as it moved along like a snake, splitting the cave in two. A blast of freezing air took Anna's breath away.

Anna bent down to examine the cleft in the floor. She could just make out an ice wall, and snow blew up into her face.

She looked up at Molly. "I think the *biome itself* is cracking. That's ice down there."

"We have to complete the circuit," Cal said. "Hank."

"What does that mean, Cal?" Molly asked.

He blew into Hank's oboe. That strange sound again. Looping up, striking the air like a silver hammer. Anna heard *click, click, click,* the sound multiplying with every second.

Click, click, click, click.

"I think I know what the apex predator is," she said as thousands of hives opened and the jawbugs emerged in an angry, clacking crowd.

31

Molly

The jawbug robots were everywhere. The air was thick with their pumping wings and glinting eyes. Their clacking jaws chomped onto Molly's flesh. She felt one trying to crawl in her ear, and screamed as she tore it out.

"Cal, what did you do?!" she bellowed.

"Stay behind me!" Yoshi yelled. He held the katana out and slashed it through the air. Molly and the others crowded in behind him as he tried to shield them. But it was too hard, and there were too many jawbugs. Dana stumbled, a mantis bug chewing on her shoulder, and Hank ripped it off and threw it away. Stu and Drew went back-to-back, waving their arms frantically to keep the cloud away from their faces. Hank threw himself on top of Dana to prevent the bugs from attacking her, then tried to help her to her feet.

The cave was suddenly moving, wrenching one way, then another, tossing them against the walls. More cracks appeared and rained down dirt. The cave was collapsing.

"Stop!" Cal ordered Yoshi. "Don't attack!"

"What are you talking about? They're killing us!" Yoshi said, his sword moving through a line of jawbugs.

Cal took out Hank's oboe and began to play. The music sailed over the noise of the cracking ground and the humming wings of the jawbugs. Their attack slowed, then stopped. The cloud rose slowly, buzzed around their heads without attacking.

"They want to complete the circuit, that's all," Cal said.

"This is a *mainframe*," Anna said with wonder, pointing to the nests on the walls. "A computer hive. Think about it. It maintains the biome and controls the time-distortion fields. The worker robots, too, probably. Maybe it's instructing the biome itself. That's not an alien device you found, Hank. It's a piece of code."

"I don't know what you mean," Hank said. "I don't even know what a mainframe is."

"Basically it's just a computer with a huge brain," Molly said. "It's where all the processing happens. Or at least a big chunk of it. There's no way to know if it's the only mainframe in the valley. But it's important enough that it programmed a massive protection device . . . thousands of jawbug robots. Am I right?" she asked Cal.

He nodded. "The Thing. You call it apex. It's a brain."

"Here's a question, though," Crash said. "Is this a good guy or a bad guy?"

Molly hugged herself, rubbing her arms. "I don't know."

"Kind of a crucial question, isn't it?"

Cal blew into the oboe again.

The jawbugs aligned themselves into a V shape and flew down the tunnel.

"Come on!" Cal shouted, and ran after them.

The team followed, slipping on the icy ground. The jawbugs now hovered near the cave walls. Molly and the others walked closer. In the middle of the back wall was a blank, six-sided shape that was slightly torqued.

"Here," Anna said. "That's where the device goes."

"Maybe if we click it in, it will stop the destruction," Molly said. The floor gave another huge lurch.

"Or it unleashes the kraken," Javi said.

"It's worth a try." Molly looked at everyone. "Agree?"

Slowly, everyone nodded. They were shaking with cold now, as the frost extended down the walls and whitened the floor.

Hank crossed to the wall with the empty hexagon. Carefully, he aligned the metal object with the space, then pressed it in. They all heard the sharp click, as if the hive itself was satisfied to have the chunk attached.

At first there was only silence, except for the lapping of water. The ground was still.

"Thank goodness," Pammy breathed. "I thought we were goners. I—"

Then they heard a crack so loud it was as if the earth itself had split. The cave suddenly tilted, throwing them forward. The floor sloped, and they began to slide.

"Circuit closed!" Cal cried gleefully. "Completion mode!"

The jawbugs winged their way back to their individual hives. The click of the hives closing was almost drowned out as water suddenly began sluicing down the cave floor. It drenched Molly's legs, and the sharp cold of it stole the breath from her lungs.

"What's happening?" Dana asked, panic in her voice.

"Malfunction of the maintenance mode," Cal said. "Danger."

"You *think*?" Javi yelled, holding on to the cave wall as the water swirled around him.

"Exit up," Cal said. He wheeled around and headed into the darkness, pumping his legs hard against the slant of the ground.

"Are we supposed to follow him?" Javi shouted. The noise of the cave almost swallowed his voice whole.

They turned and ran after Cal, trying to stay on their feet while they sloshed through the freezing water.

They caught up to find him facing a sheer blank wall.

"We're trapped," Javi said, his voice desperate.

Another great heave of the cave nearly threw Molly off her feet again. The water was now almost up to her waist and was pouring through the cracks in the ceiling.

"Buddy," Hank said. "If you can help us, the time is now."

Cal took a breath and disappeared under the water. Molly saw him swimming toward the wall, just a blur of movement beneath the surface. Swimming toward . . .

"There's an opening!" she said. "Come on."

Molly sucked in a gulp of air and plunged under. Even prepared for it, the cold of the water threatened to overwhelm her. She could see Cal stroking through a smaller tunnel. Under the water, the sounds of the cave breaking apart were muffled. She pushed toward Cal, her lungs squeezing.

The tunnel angled sharply upward. In a moment Molly saw the darkness lighten. She was able to get her head above water. Gasping, she steadied herself as her feet found the floor. Cal was already pushing through the water, climbing uphill.

She moved a few steps and looked behind her. One by one, she saw everybody surface. Crash pulled the soaked and shaken Pammy behind him. They hadn't lost anyone.

"Keep going!" she called, her voice echoing. "I see an exit!"

The air on her face felt like a blessing. She saw a square of gray sky.

Cal hoisted himself up and out of the cave. Molly followed. She stuck her head and shoulders out, then crawled upward, gulping in the warm night air. What greeted her eyes made her wonder if she was dreaming. It was as if the whole world was splitting apart.

"What is this?" Javi asked, joining her.

Below them, the stream boiled in a deep crack in the earth. Chunks of ice slammed against the walls of the fissure. If it grew much larger, it would cut them off from the forest and the compound.

But the ridge that led beyond was straight ahead.

Anna helped Akiko and Kira climb out and they struggled toward Molly and Javi. Anna paused to bend down and reach into the widening crevice.

"Anna, be careful!" Molly called.

Anna quickly lurched back, gripping something in her palm. She hurried toward them, carrying a handful of grassy strands. She held them up, showing them the thin, spiky blades.

"Look!" she said. "They're symmetrical. It's some kind of Arctic grass that was growing near the cave exit. Do you know what this means? It's *ours*! I mean, it's not manufactured! It's from Earth!"

Anna's eyes were shining. She handed the plant to Molly.

Molly shook her head tiredly. "Well, whatever's surviving there won't be for much longer." She pointed. "Look."

The split in the earth was getting wider and deeper by the minute. As the stream flowed it cut into the walls, battering them with icy chunks and crumbling them apart. The top of the cave, already split with fractures, was straining and bending. The biome was cracking like an egg.

"Get everyone out!" Molly bellowed. "We've got to get to the ridge!"

Javi scrambled toward the hole and pulled out Hank, then Dana. Yoshi emerged and reached back to grab Pammy's hand.

Molly watched in horror as a crack in the earth raced toward the cave. The ground juddered under their feet.

"HURRY!" Molly screamed, even as the floor buckled. Pammy. Stu. Drew. They all got out. With the sight of each of them, Molly's heart eased a little bit.

Then with a great roar, the cave cracked in two. They were all thrown into the air with the violence of the split.

Molly landed hard. She wasn't hurt, just stunned. She'd landed on the other side of the growing chasm.

Across the abyss, Stu, Drew, and Pammy were still on top of the other half of the cave. They'd been thrown down and were just struggling to their feet. Pammy's eyes were wide as she saw they were separated from the others. She took a faltering step forward, then glanced back, toward the compound.

"Pammy!" Dana shouted. "Come on!"

Pammy shook her head, her eyes wide with tears. "I can't . . . " she sobbed. "I don't trust their plan!"

Molly's stomach clenched when she heard the words. The crack was growing larger by the moment.

"Pammy, you have to jump *now*!" Hank yelled. "Stu, Drew—grab her and come here!"

None of the three budged.

"We're safe in the compound . . . " Drew said.

". . . And we could be doomed if we go!" Stu finished.

Pammy's face was in her hands. "I don't want to die like Dave!"

The sound of the water was like thunder. Pammy, Stu, and Drew held on to the small bits of vegetation they could grab. Molly realized that their part of the cave was sliding slowly down an incline.

They were sliding into the abyss.

The ground gave another heave, and she barely kept to her feet. She watched as a tree the size of a building crashed down across the ravine.

Pammy, Stu, and Drew used the branches to pull themselves to relative safety on higher ground, but the gulf was wider than any of them could jump.

"They'll never make it without us," Dana muttered.

She put her hand on Hank's shoulder. "Take care of the crew," she said. "Find help for Cal."

"What are you going to do? There's no way across!"

She turned to Cal, who stood with his back to them, facing the ridge. "Cal! Don't forget me," she said. "Don't forget any of us."

Cal slowly turned. He said nothing. He raised Hank's oboe. One mournful cry, something that cracked the sky.

Molly felt its meaning beat in her blood, full of sorrow. "'Friend,'" she said.

Dana began to run. That's when Molly saw she was holding the Cub-Tones' device. The one Hank used to make water cubes.

A device identical to the one the Killbots possessed.

"Dana, wait!" Kimberly cried.

Molly felt the lurch as Dana pressed down on the gravity symbol on her device.

She leaped into the air, soaring several yards forward. But Dana had never practiced with low gravity. Molly could see now that her jump had been too timid.

She landed lightly onto the tree trunk, which had formed a kind of bridge to the other half of the cave. It split and cracked even as she raced across it. The branches whipped around as it jounced, rolling at times.

"Chair step!" Kimberly shouted.

Dana lifted her legs, avoiding the branches as they shivered and twisted, hopping her way across even as the massive trunk fractured.

With a loud crack, the trunk split completely and began to fall. Dana pushed up, arcing high into the air. When she floated over the other side of the cave, she deactivated the device and went spilling hard to the ground. Stu and Drew grabbed her tightly as the tree crashed into the abyss.

Dana struggled to her feet. She looked back at them across the distance. Then she gave a little wave.

"Come back for us!" she yelled. "If you actually do find some help out there!" Then, as the ground heaved, she pressed down again on the gravity symbol. Together, Dana, Pammy, Drew, and Stu jumped to safety. They were lost from sight as they fled into the forest.

Javi

J avi and the others climbed the ridge without speaking. Whatever forest creatures had been there had migrated to wherever the mainframe had told them to go. Javi hoped it was far, *far* away.

He reached the top of the ridge as the light was fading. Just as Anna had said, they saw only more forest. At the very edge, though, there was a line of gray.

"That could be water," Molly said. She had the best eyesight of the group.

"Anybody got a boat?" Javi asked.

"One step at a time," Molly said. "Let's get a fire going. It's too late to climb down the back of the ridge."

The fire made a cheerful glow against the gray. The night wind seemed colder up here. They wrapped themselves in blankets.

Yoshi disappeared and came back with nothing. "No animals left, not even birds," he said. "Maybe we'll have more luck down there."

"It's okay," Kimberly said. "We have seed cakes."

But no one could eat. All they could think about was Dana, Pammy, Stu, and Drew heading back to the compound. How would they survive? What would their first night be like?

"Do you think the whole biome was destroyed?" Kimberly asked. Her face was taut, as if she'd been holding in the question.

"No," Yoshi said. "I think the problem was right at the seam."

"The ice and frost weren't on the other side," Anna said. "The treetops are still there. Look." She directed Kimberly's attention to the panoramic view of the forest. Through the mist, they could just make out a white line, like a scar in the earth. Beyond it the trees were blue. Unnatural for Earth, but here that meant they were alive and healthy.

"Look, we have to eat," Molly said. "The stronger we are, the sooner we'll get to the end of the valley. And the sooner we can go back for them."

They chewed on the cakes and drank water and watched as the mist took on a greenish glow. Javi could guess that meant the *midori* moon was high and bright. Was there anything more to fear tonight?

Javi looked down at the stretch of forest on the other side of the ridge—the path ahead. There could be new creatures there. And then when they got through it, there would be water. Maybe an expanse of it. Until they got to the building, or tower, or whatever it was, and faced something they were afraid to face. A hope that Pammy and the others hadn't believed in.

Anna stroked the Arctic plant she'd found, as if it were a piece of home. He guessed it was. Hank sat hugging his knees and staring back out toward the compound.

Cal sat cross-legged next to Hank, looking out, not blinking. Javi saw the green rash that snaked up his cheek, then disappeared under his shirt. A hard ridge of something ran down his back, close to his spine.

Javi leaned over to whisper to Molly. "Did you really understand Cal back there? Did he really say 'friend' when he made that sound?"

Molly's gaze was sad. "I don't know. I think so. It was a feeling more than a word. Maybe I just wanted him to. I want him to be human still."

"He is," Javi said. "I know it."

Molly didn't answer. He saw one tear leave the corner of her eye and make its way down her cheek. He knew he couldn't take away her fear.

He would take care of her, though. No matter what. No matter if she became exactly like Cal. If that was the fate that lay ahead, he would face it. He would bring her food, like Dana had for Cal. He would defend her, like Kimberly had for

Cal. He would struggle to understand her, figuring out her language, and he would speak it to her. Even if he had to learn how to play the glockenspiel.

"No matter what you are, you'll always be our leader," he said. "And you'll always be my best friend. Through everything. Even the horrible, terrible. *Especially* the horrible, terrible."

He saw her take a shuddering breath, but when she turned to him, the tear was gone.

"Enough with the mush, Perez," she said. "It's time to get some rest. We've got a long way to go."

ABOUT THE AUTHOR

Jude Watson is the author of the critically acclaimed, best-selling *Loot* and its sequel, *Sting*, along with six 39 Clues books: *Beyond the Grave, In Too Deep, Vespers Rising, A King's Ransom, Nowhere to Run*, and *Mission Titanic*. She is also the author of the bestselling Star Wars: The Last of the Jedi and Jedi Quest series. As Judy Blundell, she wrote *What I Saw and How I Lied*, the 2008 winner of the National Book Award for Young People's Literature. She lives in Long Island, New York, with her husband and daughter.

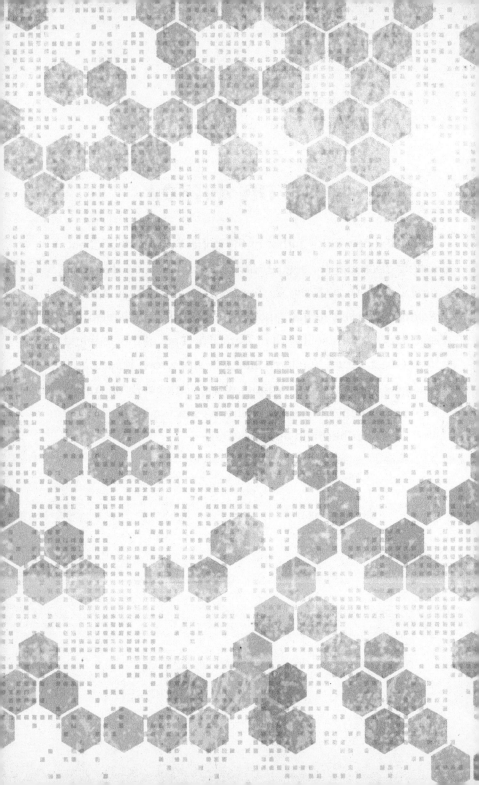

DON'T MISS

BOOK 4

BY

M.T. ANDERSON

HORIZON
THE GAME

A small group of survivors steps from
the wreckage of a plane . . .
And you're one of them.

JOIN THE RACE FOR SURVIVAL!

1. Download the app or go to **scholastic.com/horizon**
2. Log in to create your character.
3. Go to the Sequencer in your home camp.
4. Input the above musical sequence.
5. Claim your prize!